Lilian Jackson Braun composed her first poem at the age of two. She began writing her *Cat Who . . .* mysteries when one of her own Siamese cats mysteriously fell to its death from an apartment block. Since then eight *Cat Who . . .* novels have been published, all featuring the very talented Koko and Yum Yum, Siamese cats with a bent for detection. She is currently working on the next novel in the series and divides her time between her two homes in Michigan and North Carolina.

Also by Lilian Jackson Braun

1. The Cat Who Could Read Backwards
2. The Cat Who Ate Danish Modern
3. The Cat Who Turned On and Off
5. The Cat Who Played Brahms
6. The Cat Who Played Post Office
7. The Cat Who Knew Shakespeare
8. The Cat Who Sniffed Glue
9. The Cat Who Went Underground
10. The Cat Who Talked to Ghosts
11. The Cat Who Lived High
12. The Cat Who Knew a Cardinal
13. The Cat Who Moved a Mountain
14. The Cat Who Wasn't There
15. The Cat Who Went into the Closet
16. The Cat Who Came to Breakfast
17. The Cat Who Blew the Whistle
18. The Cat Who Said Cheese

The Cat Who Saw Red

Lilian Jackson Braun

First published in Great Britain 1990
by HEADLINE BOOK PUBLISHING

9

All characters in this publication are fictitious and any resemblance to real persons, living or dead, is purely coincidental.

ISBN 978-0-7472-3314-5

Printed and bound in Great Britain by
Clays Ltd, St Ives plc

HEADLINE BOOK PUBLISHING
A division of Hodder Headline PLC
338 Euston Road
London NW1 3BH

The Cat Who Saw Red

ONE

JIM QWILLERAN SLUMPED in a chair in the Press Club dining room, his six-feet-two telescoped into a picture of dejection and his morose expression intensified by the droop of his oversized mustache.

His depression had nothing to do with the price of mixed drinks, which had gone up ten cents. It had nothing to do with the dismal lighting, or the gloomy wood paneling, or the Monday mustiness that blended Friday's fish and Saturday's beer with the body odor of an old building that had once been the county jail. Qwilleran had been stunned by bad news of a more vital nature.

The prize-winning feature writer of the *Daily Fluxion* and the newspaper's foremost connoisseur of sixteen-ounce steaks and apple pie à la mode was reading—with horror and dismay—a list printed on a bilious shade of green paper.

Across the table Arch Riker, the *Fluxion*'s feature editor, said: "What's everybody going to eat today? I see they've got potato pancakes on the menu."

Qwilleran continued to stare at the sheet of green paper, adjusting his new reading glasses on his nose as if he couldn't believe they were telling him the truth.

Odd Bunsen, *Fluxion* photographer, lit a cigar. "I'm having pea soup and short ribs and an order of hash browns. But first I want a double martini."

In silence Qwilleran finished reading his incredible document and started again at the top of the list:

NO POTATOES
NO BREAD
NO CREAM SOUPS
NO FRIED FOODS

Riker, who had the comfortably upholstered contours of a newspaper deskman, said: "I want something light. Chicken and dumplings, I guess, and coleslaw with sour cream. What are you having, Qwill?"

NO GRAVY
NO SOUR CREAM
NO DESSERTS

Qwilleran squirmed in his chair and gave his fellow staffers a vinegary smirk. "I'm having cottage cheese and half a radish."

"You must be sick," Bunsen said.

"Doc Beane told me to lose thirty pounds."

"Well, you're reaching that flaky age," the photographer said cheerfully. He was younger and thinner and could afford to be philosophical.

In a defensive gesture Qwilleran stroked his large black mustache, now noticeably flecked with gray. He folded his glasses and put them in his breast pocket, handling them gingerly.

Riker, buttering a roll, looked concerned. "How come you went to the doctor, Qwill?"

"I was referred by a veterinarian." Qwilleran fumbled for his tobacco pouch and started to fill his voluptuously curved pipe. "You see, I took Koko and Yum Yum to the vet to have their teeth cleaned. Did you ever try to pry open the mouth of a Siamese cat? They think it's an outrageous invasion of privacy."

"Wish I'd been there with a movie camera," Bunsen said.

"When Koko realized what we had in mind, he turned into something like a fur tornado. The vet got him around the neck, an assistant grabbed his legs, and I hung on to his tail, but Koko turned inside out. Next thing we knew, he was off the table and headed for the kennel room, with two vets and a kennel boy chasing him around the cages. Dogs barking—cats having fits—people yelling! Koko landed on top of the air conditioner, eight feet off the floor, and looked down and gave us a piece of his mind. And if you've never been cussed out by a Siamese, you don't know what profanity is all about!"

"I know!" said Bunsen. "That cat's got a voice like an ambulance siren."

"After that episode I was bushed, and the vet said I needed a physical checkup more than the cats needed a dental prophylaxis. I've been short of breath lately, so I took his advice and went to Doc Beane."

"How'd you get the cat down?"

"We walked away and left him there, and soon he came sauntering into the examination room, hopped on the table, and yawned."

"Score another one for Koko," said Riker. "What was the female doing all this time?"

"Yum Yum was sitting in the traveling box waiting her turn."

"And probably laughing like hell," said Bunsen.

"So that's the story," Qwilleran summed up. "And that's why I'm on this miserable diet."

"You'll never stick with it."

"Oh, yes I will! I even bought a bathroom scale with some of my prize money—an antique from a country doctor's office in Ohio."

Qwilleran had won $1,000 in a *Daily Fluxion* writing contest, and the entire staff was waiting to see how the frugal bachelor would spend it.

"What did you do with the rest of the dough?" Riker asked with gentle sarcasm. "Send it to your ex-wife?"

"I sent Miriam a couple of hundred, that's all."

"You chump!"

"She's sick."

"And your in-laws are rich," Arch reminded him. "You should be buying a car for yourself—or some furniture so you can get a decent place to live."

"There's nothing wrong with my apartment in Junktown."

"I mean you should get married again—start buying a house in the suburbs—settle down."

Qwilleran cringed at the suggestion. After lunch, when the three men walked back to the office, he continued to cringe inwardly—for several reasons. In the first place, he loathed cottage cheese. Also, Riker had been goading him gently throughout the lunch hour, and Qwilleran had let him get away with it because they were old friends. The third reason for his discomfort was a summons from the managing editor to attend an afternoon meeting. An invitation from the boss was usually bad news, and the man himself riled Qwilleran; he had a synthetic camaraderie that he turned on and off to suit his purpose at the moment.

Qwilleran reported to the front office at the appointed time, accompanied by Riker, his immediate superior.

"Come in, Arch. Come in, Qwill," said the editor—in the syrupy voice he reserved for certain occasions. "Did you fellows have a good lunch? I saw you at the club living it up."

Qwilleran grunted.

The boss motioned them to seats and settled into his high-backed executive chair, beaming with magnanimity. "Qwill, we've got a new assignment for you," he said, "and I think you're going to like it."

Qwilleran's face remained impassive. He would believe it when he heard the details.

"Qwill, everyone seems to think you're the champion trencherman on the staff, and that fact per se qualifies you for a job we're creating. In addition, we know you can give us the meaty writing we're constantly striving for on this paper. We're assigning you, my friend, to the new gourmet beat."

"What's *that* all about?" The question came out gruffly.

"We want you to write a regular column on the enjoyment of good food and wine. We want you to dine at all the outstanding restaurants—on an expense account, of course. The *Fluxion* will pay expenses for two. You can take a guest." The editor paused and waited for some expression of joy.

Qwilleran merely swallowed and stared at him.

"Well, how does it sound, Qwill?"

"I don't know," Qwilleran replied slowly. "You know, I've been on the wagon for two years . . . and today I started a low-calorie diet. Doc Beane wants me to lose thirty pounds."

The boss was nonplussed for only the fraction of a second. "Naturally there's no need to *eat* everything," he said. "Just sample this and that, and use your imagination. You know the tricks of the trade. Our cooking editor can't boil an egg, but she puts out the best recipe page in the country."

"Well . . ."

"I see no reason why you can't handle it." The managing editor's brief show of goodwill was fading into his usual expression of preoccupation. "We plan to start next Monday and give the column a send-off in Sunday's paper—with your photograph and a biography. Arch tells me you've eaten all over Europe."

Qwilleran turned to his friend. "Did you know about this, Arch?"

The feature editor nodded guiltily. He said, "Better get that mustache trimmed and have a new picture taken. In your old photo you look as if you have bleeding ulcers."

The boss rose and consulted his watch. "Well, that's the story. Congratulations, Qwill!"

On the way back to the feature department Riker said, "Can't you defer that diet a few weeks? This bright idea of Percy's will blow over like all the rest of them. We're only doing it because we found out the *Morning Rampage* is starting a gourmet column in two weeks. Meanwhile, you can live like a king—entertain a different date every night—and it won't cost you a cent. That should appeal to your thrifty nature. You're Scotch, aren't you?"

"Scottish," Qwilleran grumbled. "Scotch comes in bottles."

He went first to the barber and then to the photo lab to have his picture taken and to complain to Odd Bunsen about the new assignment.

"If you need company, I'm available," the photographer volunteered. "I'll eat, and you can take notes." He seated Qwilleran on a stool in a backbreaking position and tilted his head at an unnatural angle.

"Riker says you should make me look like a bon vivant," Qwilleran said with a frown.

Bunsen squinted through the viewfinder of the portrait camera. "With that upside-down mustache you'll never look like anything but a hound dog with a bellyache. Let's have a little smile."

Qwilleran twitched a muscle in one cheek.

"Why don't you start by eating at the Toledo Tombs? That's the most expensive joint. Then you can do all the roadhouses." Bunsen stopped to twist Qwilleran's shoulders to the left and his chin to the right. "And you ought to write a column on the Heavenly Hash Houses and tell people how rotten they are."

"Who's running the gourmet column? You or me?"

"Okay, now. A little smile."

The muscle twitched again.

"You moved! We'll have to try another . . . Say, wait till your crazy cats hear about the new assignment!

Think about all the doggie bags you can take home to those brats."

"I never thought of that," Qwilleran murmured. His face brightened, and Bunsen snapped the picture.

The *Fluxion*'s new gourmet reporter had every intention of starting his tour of duty at the exclusive Toledo Tombs—although not with Odd Bunsen. He telephoned Mary Duckworth, the most glamorous name in his address book.

"I'm so sorry," she said. "I'm leaving for the Caribbean, and I've already declined an invitation to attend a Gourmet Club dinner tonight. Would you like to go in my place? You could write a column on it."

"Where's the dinner?"

"At Maus Haus. Do you know the place?"

"Mouse House?" Qwilleran repeated. "Not a very appetizing name for a restaurant."

"It's not a restaurant," Mary Duckworth explained. "It's the home of Robert Maus, the attorney. *M-a-u-s*, but he uses the German pronunciation. He's a superb cook—the kind who locks up his French knives every night, and whips up a sauce with thirty-seven ingredients from memory, and grows his own parsley. They say he can tell the right wing from the left wing of the chicken by its taste."

"Where is . . . Maus Haus?"

"On River Road. It's a weird building that's connected with a famous suicide mystery. Maybe you can solve it. Wouldn't that be a scoop for the *Daily Fluxion*?"

"When did the incident happen?"

"Oh, before I was born."

Qwilleran huffed into his mustache. "Not exactly hot news."

"Don't discuss it at the dinner table," Mary warned. "Robert is thoroughly weary of the subject. I'll phone and tell him you'll be there."

Qwilleran went home early that afternoon to change into his good suit and to feed the cats, first stopping at the grocery to buy them some fresh meat. With their catly perception they knew he was coming even before he climbed the stairs. Waiting for him, they looked like two loaves of homemade bread. They sat facing the door—two bundles of pale toasty fur with brown legs tucked out of sight. But the brown ears were alert, and two pairs of blue eyes questioned the man who walked into the apartment.

"Greetings," he said. "I'm early tonight. And wait till you kids see what I've brought you!"

The two cats rose as one. "Yow!" said Koko in a chesty baritone. "Mmmm!" said Yum Yum in a soprano squeal of rapture.

She leaped on the unabridged dictionary and started scratching its tattered cover for joy, while Koko sailed onto the desk in a demonstration of effortless levitation and stepped on the tabulator key of the typewriter, making the carriage jump.

Qwilleran stroked each cat in turn, massaging Koko's silky back with a heavy hand and caressing Yum Yum's paler fur with tenderness. "How's the little sweetheart?" He spoke to Yum Yum with an unabashed gentleness that his cronies at the Press Club would not have believed and that no woman in his life had ever heard.

"Chicken livers tonight," he told the cats, and Koko expressed his approval by resetting the lefthand margin on the typewriter. His mechanical ability was a newfound talent. He could operate wall switches and open doors, but most of all he was fascinated by the typewriter with its abundance of levers, knobs, and keys.

Qwilleran had mentioned this development to the veterinarian, who had said, "Animals go through phases of interest, like children. How old are the cats?"

"I have no idea. They were both full-grown when I adopted them."

"Koko is probably three or four. Very healthy. And he seems highly intelligent."

At this comment Qwilleran had smoothed his mustache discreetly and refrained from mentioning Koko's outstanding faculty. The truth was that the precocious Siamese seemed to possess uncanny skills of detection.

Qwilleran had recently uncovered a crime that baffled the police, and only his close friends knew that Koko was largely responsible for solving the case.

Qwilleran chopped chicken livers for the cats, warmed them in a little broth, and arranged the delicacy on a plate the way they liked it, with juices puddling in the center and bite-size morsels of meat around the rim.

"Lucky beggars!" he said. They could eat all they wanted without gaining an ounce. Under their sleek fawn-colored fur they were lean and muscular. Although they moved with grace and feather-light tread, there was strength in their hind legs that carried them to the top of the refrigerator in a single effortless leap.

Qwilleran watched them for a while and then turned his attention to his new assignment, sitting down at the typewriter to make a list of restaurants. He always left a fresh sheet of paper in position around the platen, ready for action—a writer's trick that made it easier to get started—and as he glanced at this paper, his fingers halted over the keys. He put on his new glasses and had a closer look. There was a single letter typed at the top of the page.

"By golly, I knew you'd learn to operate this machine sooner or later," he said over his shoulder, and there was a gargled response from the kitchen, as Koko simultaneously swallowed a bit of liver and made an offhand comment.

It was a capital *T*. The keyboard was locked in upper case. Koko had apparently stepped on the shift lock with his left paw and on the letter key with his right.

Qwilleran added "oledo Tombs" to Koko's *T* and then listed the Golden Lamb Chop, the Medium Rare Room at the Stilton Hotel, and several roadhouses, ethnic restaurants, and underground bistros.

Then he dressed for dinner, shedding the tweed sports coat, the red plaid tie, the gray button-down shirt, and the dust-colored slacks that constituted his uniform at the *Daily Fluxion*. In doing so, he caught a glimpse of himself in the full-length mirror, and what he saw he did not like. His face was fleshed out; his upper arms were flabby; where he should have been concave, he was convex.

Hopefully but not confidently he stepped on the antique scale in the bathroom. It was a rusty contraption with weights and a balance arm, and the arm went up with a sharp clunk. He held his breath and moved the weight along the arm, hesitantly adding a quarter-pound, a half-pound, then one, two, three pounds before the scale was in balance. Three pounds! He had eaten nothing but grapefruit for breakfast and cottage cheese for lunch and he was three pounds heavier than he had been that morning.

Qwilleran was appalled—then discouraged—then angry. "Dammit!" he said aloud. "I'm not going to turn into a fat slob for the sake of a lousy assignment!"

"Yow!" said Koko by way of encouragement.

Qwilleran stepped off the scale to take another critical look in the mirror, and the sight sent a wave of determination surging through his flabby flesh. He expanded his chest, sucked in his waistline, and felt a new strength of character.

"I'll write that damn column," he announced to the cats, "and I'll stay on that dumb diet if it kills me!"

"Yow-wow!" said Koko.

"Three pounds heavier! I can't believe it!"

While weighing himself, Qwilleran had failed to notice Koko standing behind him with front paws planted solidly on the platform of the scale.

TWO

As Jim Qwilleran dressed for dinner Monday evening, he was feeling his age. He now needed reading glasses for the first time in his life; his mustache and good head of hair had now reached the pepper-and-salt stage; and his beefy waistline was another reminder of his forty-six years. But before the evening was over, he was a young man again.

He took a taxi to the River Road residence of Robert Maus—out beyond a sprawling shopping center, beyond Joe Pike's Seafood Hut with its acres of parking, beyond a roller rink and lumberyard. Between a marina and a tennis club stood a monstrous pile of stone. Qwilleran had seen it before and guessed it to be the lodge hall of some eccentric cult. It stood back from the highway, aloof and mysterious behind its iron fence and two acres of neglected lawn, resembling an Egyptian temple that had been damaged in transit and ineptly repaired.

Pylons framed a massive door that might have been excavated on the Nile, but other architectural features were absurdly out of character: Georgian chimneys, large factory windows in the upper story, an attached garage on one side and a modern carport on the other, and numerous fire escapes, ledges, and eaves troughs in all the wrong places.

Qwilleran found a door knocker and let it fall with a resounding clang. Then he waited—with an air of resignation, his stomach growling its hunger—until the heavy door opened on creaking hinges.

For the next half-hour very little made sense. Qwilleran was greeted by a slender young man with impudent eyes and ridiculous sideburns, long and curly. Although he wore the white duck coat of a servant, he was carrying a half-empty champagne glass in one hand and a cigarette in the other, and he was grinning like a cat in a tree. "Welcome to Maus Haus," he said. "You must be the guy from the newspaper."

Qwilleran stepped into the dim cavern that was the foyer.

"Mickey Maus is in the kitchen," said the official greeter. "I'm William." He lipped his cigarette in order to thrust his right hand forward.

Qwilleran shook hands with the amiable houseboy or butler or whatever he was. "Just William?"

"William Vitello."

The newsman looked sharply at the young-old leprechaun face. "Vitello? I could swear you were Irish."

"Irish mother, Italian father. My whole family is a goulash," William explained with an ear-to-ear smile. "Come on in. Everybody's in the Great Hall, getting crocked, I'll introduce you around."

He led the way into a vast hall so dark that scores of lamps and candles on torchères and in sconces succeeded in lighting it only dimly, but Qwilleran could distinguish a balcony supported by Egyptian columns and a grand staircase guarded by sphinxes. The floor and walls were inlaid with ceramic tiles in chocolate brown, and voices bounced off the slick surfaces, resounding with eerie distortions.

"Spooky place, if you don't mind my saying so," said Qwilleran.

"You don't know the half of it," William informed him. "It's a real turkey."

In the center of the hall, under the lofty ceiling, a long table was laid for dinner, but the guests were cocktailing under the balcony, where there was some degree of coziness.

"Champagne or sherry?" William asked. "The sherry's a bomb, I ought to warn you."

"You can skip the drink," Qwilleran said, reaching in his pocket for tobacco and pipe and hoping that a smoke would curb his hunger pangs.

"It's just a small party tonight. Most of the people live here. Want to meet some of the girls?" William jerked his head in the direction of two brunettes.

"*Live* here! What kind of establishment is Maus running?"

The houseboy hooted with delight. "Didn't you know? This is a sort of weird boarding house. It used to be a real art center—studios on the balcony and a big pottery operation in the back—but that was before Mickey Maus took it over. I'm a charity case myself. I go to art school and get room and board in exchange for several kinds of menial and backbreaking labor."

"Of which grass-cutting is not one," Qwilleran said with a nod toward the shaggy front lawn.

William launched another explosive laugh and slapped the newsman on the back. "Come and meet Hixie and Rosemary. But look out for Hixie; she's a husband-hunter."

The two women were standing near a sideboard that held platters of hors d'oeuvres. Rosemary Whiting was a nice-looking woman of indefinite age and quiet manner. Hixie Rice was younger, plumper, louder, and had longer eyelashes.

Hixie was intently busy with her champagne-sipping and canapé-nibbling, all the while chattering in a high-pitched monotone: "I'm rabid for chocolate! Chocolate butter creams, chocolate chip cookies, brownies, black-bottom pie, devil's food cake—anything that's made with chocolate and three cups of sugar and a pound of butter." She stopped to pop a bacon-wrapped oyster into her mouth.

There was quite a lot of Hixie, Qwilleran noted. Her figure ballooned out wherever her tightly fitted orange dress would permit, and her hair puffed like a chocolate soufflé above her dimpled dumpling face.

"Caviar?" Rosemary murmured to Qwilleran, offering a platter.

He took a deep breath and resolutely declined.

"It's rich in vitamin D," she added.

"Thanks just the same."

"Mickey Maus," William was saying, "is a nut about butter. The only time he ever lost his cool was when we were having a small brunch and we were down to our last three pounds of butter. He panicked."

"Unfortunately, animal fats—" Rosemary began in a soft voice, but she was interrupted by Hixie.

"I eat a lot because I'm frustrated, but I'd rather be fat and jolly than thin and crabby. You have to admit that I have a delightful disposition." She batted her eyelashes and reached for another canapé. "What's on the menu tonight, Willie?"

"Not much. Just cream of watercress soup, jellied clams, stuffed breast of chicken baked in a crust, braised endive—I hate endive—broiled curried tomatoes, romaine salad, and crepes suzette."

"That's what Charlotte would call just a little bite to eat," Hixie observed.

William explained to Qwilleran: "Charlotte never has a meal. Only what she calls 'a bite to eat.' That's Charlotte over there—the old gal with the white hair and five pounds of jewelry."

The woman with hair like spun sugar was talking vehemently to two paunchy gentlemen who were listening with more politeness than interest. Qwilleran recognized them as the Penniman brothers, members of the Civic

Arts Commission. It was Penniman money that had founded the *Morning Rampage*, endowed the art school, and financed the city park system.

Moving nervously about the Great Hall was another man who looked vaguely familiar. He had a handsome face and a brooding expression that changed to a dazzling smile whenever a woman glanced his way; the startling feature of his appearance was a shaven head.

Qwilleran, studying the other guests, noted an attractive redhead in an olive green pantsuit . . . and a young man with a goatee . . . and then he saw *her*. For a moment he forgot to breathe.

Impossible! he told himself. And yet there was no mistaking that tiny figure, that heavy chestnut hair, that provocative one-sided smile.

At the same time, she turned in his direction and stared in disbelief. He felt a crawling sensation on his upper lip, and he touched his mustache. She started to move toward him across the tile floor—gliding the way she used to do, her dress fluttering the way it used to do, her melodic voice calling, "Jim Qwilleran! Is it really you?"

"Joy! Joy Wheatley!"

"I can't believe it!" She stared at him and then rushed into his arms.

"Let me look at you, Joy . . . You haven't changed a bit."

"Oh, yes, I have."

"How many years has it been?"

"Please don't add them up . . . I like your mustache, Jim, and you're huskier than you were."

"You mean stouter. You're being kind. You were always kind."

She pulled away. "Not always. I'm ashamed of what I did."

He looked at her closely and felt his collar tighten. "I never thought I'd see you again, Joy. What are you doing here?"

"We've been living here since January. My husband

and I operate the pottery at the back of the building."

"You're married?" Qwilleran's rising hopes leveled off.

"My name is Graham now. What are you doing here, Jim?"

"No one calls me Jim anymore. I've been Qwill for the last twenty years."

"Do you still spell Qwilleran with a *w*?"

"Yes, and it still gives typesetters and proofreaders ulcers."

"Married?"

"Not at the moment."

"Are you still writing?"

"I've been with the *Daily Fluxion* for more than a year. Haven't you noticed my byline?"

"I'm not much of a reader—don't you remember? And my husband is mad at the *Fluxion* art critic, so he buys the *Morning Rampage*."

"Tell me, Joy—where have you been all these years?"

"Mostly in California—until Mr. Maus invited us to come here and take charge of the pottery . . . There's so much to talk about! We'll have to—when can we—?"

"Joy," Qwilleran said, lowering his voice, "why did you run away?"

She sighed and looked first to one side and then the other. "I'll explain later, but first I think you should meet my husband . . . before the terrible-tempered Mr. G. throws a tantrum," she added with a wry smile.

Qwilleran looked across the hall and saw a tall, angular man watching them. Dan Graham had faded carrot hair, a prominent Adam's apple, and freckled skin stretched taut across prominent bones in his face and hands. His worn corduroy jacket, unpressed shirt, and barefoot sandals evidently were intended to express the free artistic spirit, Qwilleran thought, but instead they made the man look seedy and forlorn. But terrible-tempered? . . . No.

Graham's nod of acknowledgment was curt when Joy introduced Qwilleran as "an old flame." There was something pointed about the way she said it—not with mischief but with spite—and Qwilleran thought, All is not well between these two. And he felt guilty about feeling glad.

He said to Dan Graham, "I knew your wife in Chicago when we were kids. I was the boy next door. I'm with the *Daily Fluxion* now."

Graham mumbled something. He spoke rapidly and swallowed his words.

"Beg your pardon?" Qwilleran said.

"Gettingreadyforanexhibition. Maybeyoucangetme somepublicity."

Joy said, "It's going to be a husband-and-wife show. We work in quite different styles. I hope you'll attend the opening, Jim."

"Don'tthinkmuchofyourartcritic," her husband mumbled. "Hisreviewsaren'tworthahillofbeans."

"Nobody loves an art critic," Qwilleran said. "That's one newspaper job I wouldn't want. Otherwise, how do you like it here in the Midwest, Mr. Graham?"

"Wouldn't give you two cents for this town," said the potter. Qwilleran's ear was becoming attuned to his rapid delivery and his liberal use of outdated expressions and clichés. "Expect to work in New York eventually—maybe Europe."

"Well, I like this part of the country very much," Joy said defiantly. "I'd like to stay here." She had always liked everything very much. Qwilleran remembered her boundless enthusiasms.

Graham glanced testily at the dinner table. "Jeepers creepers! When do we get some chow? I could eat a horse." He waved an empty champagne glass. "This stuff gives you an appetite and no buzz."

"Do you realize," Qwilleran asked, "that I haven't met our host?"

Joy seized his hand. "You haven't? I'll take you to the kitchen. Robert Maus is a real lamb pie."

She led him through a low-ceilinged corridor at the rear of the Great Hall, gripping his fingers and staying closer to him than was necessary. They walked in self-conscious silence.

The kitchen was a large picturesque room, fragrant with herbs and cooking wine. With its ceramic tile floor, beamed ceiling, and walk-in fireplace, it reminded Qwilleran of kitchens he had seen in Normandy. Copper pots and clusters of dried dill and rosemary hung from an overhead rack, while knives and cleavers were lined up in an oak knife block. On open shelves stood omelet pans, soufflé dishes, copper bowls, a fish poacher, salad baskets, and a few culinary objects that remained a mystery to the uninitiated.

Dominating the scene was a towering, well-built man of middle age, immaculate in white shirt, conservative tie, and gold cuff links. He had the dignity of a Supreme Court justice, plus a slight stoop that gave the effect of a gracious bow. A towel was tied around his waist, and he was kneading dough.

When Joy Graham made the introduction, Robert Maus exhibited his floured hands in apology and said in measured tones, after some consideration, "How . . . do you do."

He was assisted by a woman in a white uniform, to whom he gave brief orders in a deferential tone: "Refrigerate, if you please . . . Prepare the sauteuse, if you will . . . And now the chicken, Mrs. Marron. Thank you."

He started boning chicken breasts with deft slashes of a murderous knife.

Qwilleran said, "You handle that weapon with a vengeance."

Maus breathed heavily before replying. "I find it most . . . satisfying." He whipped the knife through the flesh, then gave the quivering breast a whack with the flat of the blade. "Shallots, if you please, Mrs. Marron."

"This is an extraordinary building," Qwilleran remarked. "I've never seen anything like it."

The attorney considered the comment at length before rendering his verdict. "It would not be unreasonable to describe it . . . as an architectural horror," he said. "With all due respect to the patron of the arts who built it, one must concede . . . that his enthusiasm and resources outweighed his . . . aesthetic awareness."

"But the apartments upstairs are adorable," Joy said. "May I take Jim to the balcony, Mr. Maus?"

He nodded graciously. "If it is your pleasure. I am inclined to believe . . . that the door to Number Six . . . is unlocked."

Qwilleran had never seen anything to equal Number Six. The studio apartment they entered was a full two stories high, and half the outer wall was window, composed of many small panes. The orange glow from a spring sunset was flooding the room with color, and three small leaded-glass windows above the desk were making their own rainbows.

Qwilleran blew into his mustache. "I like this furniture!" It was massive, almost medieval in appearance—heavily carved and reinforced with wrought iron.

"It belongs to Ham Hamilton," Joy told him. "Sexy, isn't it? He'll be sending for it as soon as he knows where he's going to be situated."

"You mean he's moved out?"

"He was transferred to Florida. He's a food buyer for a grocery chain."

Qwilleran eyed the apartment avidly—particularly the big loungy chair in bold black-and-white plaid, the row of built-in bookcases, and—wonder of wonder—a white bearskin rug. "Is this place for rent?" he asked.

The question made Joy's eyes dance. "Oh, Jim! Are you interested? Would you like to live here?"

"It would depend on the rent—and a couple of other things." He was thinking about Koko and Yum Yum.

"Let's ask Mr. Maus right away."

That was the Joy he remembered—all instant decision and breathless action.

"No, let's wait until after dinner. Let me think about it."

"Oh, Jim," she cried, throwing her arms around him. "I've thought about you so much—throughout the years."

He felt her heart beating, and he whispered, "Why

did you disappear? Why did you leave me like that? Why didn't you ever write and explain?"

She drew away. "It's a long story. We'd better go down to dinner now." And she gave him the half-smile that never failed to make his heart somersault.

The table was laid with heavy ceramic plates and pewter serving pieces on the bare oak boards, and it was lighted by candles in massive wrought-iron candelabra. Qwilleran found his place card between Hixie Rice and the white-haired woman, who introduced herself as Charlotte Roop. Joy sat at the far end of the table between Basil and Bayley Penniman, and the only way she could communicate with Qwilleran was with her eyes.

Opposite him sat the bald brute with the facile smile. The man half rose and bowed across the table with his right hand over his heart. "I'm Max Sorrel."

"Jim Qwilleran of the *Daily Fluxion*. Haven't I met you somewhere?"

"I have a restaurant. The Golden Lamb Chop."

"Yes, I had dinner there once."

"Did you order our rack of lamb? That's our specialty. We lose money on every one we serve." As the restaurateur spoke, he was industriously polishing his silverware with his napkin.

Spoons were raised. Qwilleran tasted the watercress soup and found it delicately delicious, yet he had no overwhelming desire to finish it. A sense of elation had banished his appetite. His thoughts, and his eyes, kept turning to Joy. Now he knew why he had always been attracted to women with translucent skin and long hair. Tonight Joy's luxuriant brown hair was braided and coiled around her head like a crown. Her dress had the same filmy quality he used to tease her about when she bought curtain remnants and made them into romantic, impractical clothes. What a crazy kid she had been!

William removed the soup bowls from the right, served the clams from the left, and poured a white wine, while whistling a tune off-key. When he had finished serving, he joined the guests at the table, white coat and all, and monopolized the conversation in his immediate vicinity.

"Unorthodox arrangement," Qwilleran mentioned to Hixie.

"Robert is very permissive," she said. "He seems stuffy, but he's a doll, really. May I have some more butter, please?"

"How do you happen to be living here?"

"I'm a copywriter at an agency that handles food accounts. You have to have some special interest in food, or Robert won't rent to you. Miss Roop manages a restaurant."

"Yes, I manage one of the Heavenly Hash Houses," said the woman on Qwilleran's left, twisting her several bracelets. She was a small, sprightly woman, probably nearing retirement age, and she wore an abundance of nondescript costume jewelry. "I went to work for Mr. Hashman almost forty years ago. Before that I was secretary to the late Mr. Penniman, so I know something about the newspaper business. I admire newspaper people! They're so clever with words . . . Maybe you can help me." She drew a crossword puzzle from the outer pocket of her enormous handbag. "Do you know a five-letter word for *love* that begins with *a*?"

"Try *a-g-a-p-e*," Qwilleran suggested.

Miss Roop frowned. "Agape?"

"It's a Greek word, pronounced *ag-a-pe*."

"Oh, my!" she said. "You are brilliant!" Delightedly she penciled the word in the vertical squares.

The chicken was served, and again Qwilleran found it easy to abstain. He toyed with his food and listened to the voices around him.

"Do you realize truffles are selling for seventy-five dollars a pound?" Sorrel remarked.

The redhead was saying, "Mountclemens was a fraud, you know. His celebrated lobster bisque was a quickie made with *canned* ingredients."

"I'm having so much fun in the attic of this building. I've found some old letters and notebooks stuffed away in a dusty jardiniere," Joy told Basil Penniman.

Rosemary Whiting said, "You can put a sprinkle of wheat germ in almost anything, and it's so good for you."

"Everyone knows shrimp cocktail is déclassé!" Hixie announced.

The redhead went on talking: "I know of one cassoulet that cooked for thirty years."

And Joy added, "You'd be surprised what I've found in the attic. It would upset quite a few people."

The man with the goatee was revealing a cooking secret: "I always grate cheese by hand; a little grated knuckle in the Asiago improves the flavor."

Maus himself, at the head of the table, was speechless in a world of his own making, as he tasted each dish critically, gazing into space and savoring with lips and tongue. Once he spoke: "The *croûte*, in my opinion, is a trifle too short."

"On the contrary, it's exquisite," Miss Roop assured him. She turned to Qwilleran. "Mr. Maus is a brilliant cook. He's discovered a way to roast a suckling pig without removing the eyeballs. Imagine!"

"Are you people aware," Qwilleran asked, raising his voice to attract general attention, "that Mrs. Graham also is an excellent cook? She invented a banana split cake when she was seventeen and won a statewide baking contest."

Joy blushed attractively. "It was an adolescent's delight, I'm afraid—with bananas, coconut, strawberries, chocolate, walnuts, marshmallows, *and* whipped cream."

"I don't know about her cooking," said Max Sorrel, "but she's a helluva good potter. She made this dinner service." He tapped his plate with his fork.

"It was very generous of Mr. Maus to give me such a wonderful commission," Joy said.

Qwilleran looked at the thick-textured plates of silvery gray, flecked and rimmed with brown. "You mean you made all these dishes? By hand? How many?"

"A complete service for twenty-four."

Sorrel flashed his winning smile at her. "They're terrific, honey. If I were a millionaire, I'd let you make all the dishes for my restaurant."

"You're very sweet, Max."

"How long did the job take?" Qwilleran asked.

"Hmmm . . . it's hard to say—" Joy began.

"That's nothing," Dan Graham interrupted in a voice that was suddenly loud. "Out on the Coast I did a six-hundred-piece set for one of the movie big shots."

His pronouncement had a dampening effect on the conversation. All heads immediately bent over salads. Suddenly everyone was intent on spearing romaine.

"Tell you something else," Graham persisted. "Wedgwood made nine hundred and sixty-two pieces for Catherine of Russia!"

There was silence at the table until William said, "Anyone for bridge after dinner? It'll take your mind off your heartburn."

THREE

WHEN QWILLERAN WENT home and told his widowed landlady he was moving, she cried a little, and when he gave her a month's rent in lieu of notice, Mrs. Cobb shed a few more tears.

The rent at Maus Haus was higher than he had been paying on Zwinger Street, but he told himself that the sophisticated cuisine was appropriate to his new assignment and that the cats would enjoy the bearskin rug. Yet he was fully aware of his real reason for moving.

The cats were asleep on the daybed when he went into his old apartment, and he waked them with stroking. Koko, without opening his eyes, licked Yum Yum's nose; Yum Yum licked Koko's right ear; Koko licked a paw, which happened to be his own; and Yum Yum licked Qwilleran's hand with her sandpaper tongue. He gave them some jellied clams from Maus Haus, and then he phoned Arch Riker at home.

"Arch, I hope I didn't get you out of bed," he said.

"You'll never guess who walked back into my life again tonight . . . Joy!"

There was an incredulous pause at the other end of the line. "Not Joy Wheatley!"

"She's Joy Graham now. She's married."

"What's she—? Where did you see—?"

"She and her husband are artists, and they've come here from California."

"Joy's an *artist*?"

"They do ceramics. They live in a pottery on River Road, and I'm taking an apartment in the same building."

"Careful," Arch warned.

"Don't jump to conclusions. It's all over as far as I'm concerned."

"How does she look?"

"Fine! Cute as ever. And she's the same impetuous girl. Act now, think later."

"Did she explain what—or why—?"

"We didn't have that much time to talk."

"Well, that's a bombshell! Wait till I wake up Rosie and tell her!"

"See you tomorrow around noon." Qwilleran said. "I want to stop at Kipper and Fine on my way to the office and look at their spring suits. I could use some new clothes."

He whipped off his tie and sank into an easy chair and dredged up whimsical memories: Joy baking bread in her aunt's kitchen and losing a Band-Aid in the dough; Joy getting her long hair caught in the sewing machine. As a boy he had written poems about her: Joy . . . coy . . . alloy. Qwilleran shook his head. It was incredible.

On Tuesday morning—a day that smelled joyously of spring—he spent some of his prize money on a new pair of shoes and a suit in a cut more fashionable than he had owned for some time. At noon he lunched with Arch Riker, reminiscing about old times in Chicago when they were both cub reporters, double-dating Joy and Rosie. In the afternoon he borrowed a station wagon from an antique dealer and moved his belongings to Maus Haus.

Koko and Yum Yum traveled in a canned soup carton with air holes punched in the sides, and all during the journey the box rocked and thumped and resounded with the growls and hisses of feline mayhem. Koko, a master of strategy, went through the motions of murdering Yum Yum whenever he wanted to attract urgent attention, and the little female was a willing accomplice, but Qwilleran knew their act and was no longer deceived.

Mrs. Marron, the housekeeper, admitted Qwilleran and the soup carton to Maus Haus. She was a sad-faced woman with dull eyes and a sallow complexion. With weary step she led the way across the Great Hall, now flooded with daylight from a skylight three stories overhead.

"I gave Number Six a good cleaning," she said. "William washed the walls last week. He'll bring your things up when he comes home from school."

The afternoon sun was streaming through the huge studio window as if to prove the spotlessness of the premises. The floor of brown ceramic tile gleamed with an iridescent patina; the dark oak furniture was polished; the windowpanes sparkled. Mrs. Marron lowered the Roman shade—a contraption of pleated canvas favored by artists in earlier days—and said, "Mr. Maus didn't tell me what meals you'd be taking. Everybody works different hours. They come and they go. They eat or they don't eat."

"I'll have breakfast and notify you from day to day about the other meals," Qwilleran said. "Count me in for dinner tonight . . . How about this telephone? Is it connected?"

"I'll tell the phone company to start service." She suddenly jumped back. "Oh! What's in that box?"

The soup carton, which Qwilleran had placed on the desk, had gone into convulsions, quaking and rocking and emitting unearthly sounds.

"I have two Siamese cats," the newsman explained,

"and I want to be sure they don't get out of the apartment, Mrs. Marron."

"Are they expensive?"

"They're extremely important to me, and I don't want anything to happen to them. Please be careful when you come in to clean."

When the housekeeper left, Qwilleran closed the door, first testing the lock and the latch. He also investigated the catches on the three small casement windows over the desk. He checked the bathroom window, heat registers, air vents, and anything else that might serve as an escape hatch for a determined cat. Only then did he open the soup carton.

The cats emerged cautiously, swinging their heads from side to side. Then with one accord they crept toward the white bear rug, stalking it with tails dipped and bellies close to the floor. When the beast made no move to attack or retreat, Koko bravely put his head inside the gaping jaws. He sniffed the teeth and stared into the glass eyes. Yum Yum stepped daintily on the pelt, and soon she was rolling over and over on the white fur in apparent ecstasy.

Qwilleran's practiced eye perused the apartment for trouble spots and found it catproof. His inquisitive roommates would not be able to burrow into the box spring; the bed was a captain's bunk, built in between two large wardrobes. There were no plants for Yum Yum to chew. The lamp on the desk was weighty enough to remain upright during a cat chase.

For entertainment there were pigeons on the ledge outside the windows, and an oak dining table in a sunny spot would hold the cats' blue cushion.

"I think this place will do," Qwilleran said to the cats. "Don't you?"

The answer came from the bathroom, where Koko was crowing in exultation, enjoying the extra resonance that tile walls gave to his normally loud and penetrating voice.

The man felt exhilarated, too. In fact, his elation had acted as a substitute for calories at lunchtime. Since meeting Joy the night before, his hunger pangs had vanished, and already he felt thinner. He wondered whether Joy was in the pottery—and whether it would be discreet to go looking for her—and whether he would see her at the dinner table.

Then he remembered the can of boned chicken in his topcoat pocket. He found a can opener in the tiny kitchenette and was arranging morsels of chicken on a handmade stoneware plate when he heard a knock at the door. It was a playful knock. Was it Joy? Hastily he placed the dish on the bathroom floor, summoned the cats, and closed the door on them. Before answering the knock, he took time to glance in the bathroom mirror, straighten his tie, and run a hand over his hair. With his face pleasantly composed, he flung open the door.

"Hi!" said William, who stood there grinning and carrying a suitcase and a carton of books.

"Oh, it's you," said Qwilleran, his face relaxing into its usual sober lines. "Thanks. Just drop them anywhere."

"You've got the best setup in the whole building," the houseboy said, walking around the room with a proprietary swagger. "How much rent is Mickey Maus charging you?"

"There are some more boxes in the wagon," Qwilleran told him. "And a scale, and a big wrought-iron coat of arms. Do you mind bringing them up?" He started unpacking books, stacking them in the row of built-in bookcases at one end of the room.

William walked to the window. "You've got a good view. You'll be able to watch all the wild parties down at the marina . . . Do you play bridge?"

"I'm no asset to the game," Qwilleran mumbled.

"Hey, do you really read all this heavy stuff?" The houseboy had picked up a volume of Toynbee that Qwilleran had bought for a dime at a flea market. "All I ever read is whodunits . . . Jeez! What's that?"

An earsplitting shriek came from the bathroom.

"One of the cats. Their litter pan is in the car, too, and a sack of gravel. Better bring those up first."

"Mind if I take a look at them?" William moved toward the bathroom.

"Let's wait till everything's moved in," Qwilleran said with a touch of impatience. "They might dart out into the hall. They're edgy in a strange place."

"It must be great—working for a newspaper. Do you cover murder trials?"

"Not anymore. That's not my beat."

"What do you do, then?"

Qwilleran was half irritated, half amused. The houseboy's curiosity and persistence reminded him of his own early days as a copyboy. "Look, I'll tell you the story of my life tomorrow," he said. "First let's get my things moved in. Then I'd like to visit the pottery."

"They don't like visitors," William said. "Not when they're working. Of course, if you don't mind getting thrown out on your ear . . ."

Qwilleran did not see Joy until dinnertime. The meal was served at a big round table in a corner of the kitchen, because there were only six sitting down to dinner. Robert Maus was absent, and Miss Roop and Max Sorrel were on duty at their restaurants.

The room was heady with aromas: roast beef, cheese, logs burning in the fireplace, and Joy's spicy perfume. She looked more appealing than ever, having rouged her cheeks and darkened her eyelids.

Qwilleran merely sampled the corn chowder, ate half of his portion of roast beef and broccoli parmigiana, declined a Parker House roll, and ignored a glob of mush flecked with green.

"Everything's good," he assured Mrs. Marron, who had prepared the meal, "but I'm trying to lose weight."

Rosemary, the quiet one, glanced at the untouched glob on Qwilleran's salad plate. "You should eat the bulgur. It's highly nutritious."

"Do you cook, Mr. Qwilleran?" Hixie asked.

"Only a few gourmet dishes for my cats."

The conversation at the table was lagging; the Grahams were moody, and William was eating as if he might never have another meal. Qwilleran tried to entertain the group with tales about Koko and Yum Yum. "They can smell through the refrigerator door," he said. "If there's lobster in there, they won't eat chicken, and if there's chicken, they won't eat beef. Salmon has to be a nationally advertised brand; don't ask me how they know. In the morning Koko rings for his breakfast; he steps on the tabulator key of the typewriter, which jerks the carriage and rings the bell. One of these days I think he'll learn to type."

With Joy in the audience he was feeling at his best, and yet the more he talked, the more he sensed her melancholy.

Finally she said, "I had a cat, but he disappeared a couple of weeks ago. I miss him terribly. His name was Raku."

Her husband spoke for the first time that evening. "Somebody probably stole the Blimp. That's what I called him. The Blimp." He looked pleased with himself.

"What kind of cat?" Qwilleran asked Joy. "Did you let him go out?"

"No, but cats have a way of sneaking out. He was a big smoky brown longhair."

Her husband said, "People steal cats and sell them to labs for experiments."

Joy gritted her teeth. "For God's sake, Dan, must you bring that subject up again?"

"It's getting to be big business," he said. "*Kit*napping." Dan looked hopefully around the table for appreciation of his bon mot.

"That's not funny!" Joy had put down her fork and was sitting with clenched fists. "It's not funny at all."

Qwilleran turned to her husband. "By the way, I'd like to have a tour of the pottery when you have time."

"Not before the exhibition," said the potter, shaking his head gravely.

"Why not?" his wife snapped.

"Cripes, you know it's nerve-racking to have somebody around when you're working." To Qwilleran he said, "Can't afford any interruptions. Busy as a one-armed paperhanger with the itch, if you know what I mean."

Joy turned to Qwilleran, her voice icy. "Anytime you want to see the pottery, let me know. I'd love to show you my latest work." She shot a venomous glance at her husband.

To cover the embarrassed silence that followed, the newsman addressed Graham again. "You were telling me you didn't like the *Fluxion* critic. What's your complaint?"

"He doesn't know beans about pottery, if you know what I mean."

"He was a museum curator before he started writing for us."

Graham snorted. "Doesn't mean a thing. He may know Flemish painting and African sculpture, but what he doesn't know about contemporary pots would fill a book, if you know what I mean. When I had my last one-man show in L.A., the leading critic said my textures were a treat for the eye and a thrill for the fingertips. And I quote."

Joy said to Qwilleran with a disdainful edge to her voice, "Dan put a couple of old pots in a group show when we first came here, and your critic was unkind."

"I don't expect a critic to be kind," her husband said, his Adam's apple moving rapidly. "I expect him to know his business."

William spoke up. "He calls 'em the way he sees 'em. That's all any critic can do. I think he's pretty perceptive."

"Oh, William, shut up," Joy snapped. "You don't know anything about pots either."

"I *beg* your pardon!" said the houseboy with mock indignation.

"Anyone who gets the cones mixed up and puts cracked biscuit shelves away with the good ones is a lousy potter," she said curtly.

"Well, Dan told me to—"

"Don't listen to Dan. He's as sloppy as you are. What

do they teach you at Penniman Art School? How to make paper flowers?"

Qwilleran had never seen that side of Joy's nature. She had been moody as a girl but never sharp-tongued.

Hixie said to the houseboy in a bantering tone, "Don't let it burn you, Willie dear. Your personal charm makes up for your stupidity."

"Gee, thanks."

"This bickering," Rosemary murmured, "is not very good for the digestion."

"Don't blame it on me," said William. "She started it."

Dan stood up and threw his napkin on the table. "I've had it up to the ears! Lost my appetite." He strode away from the table.

"The big baby!" his wife muttered. "I noticed he finished his apple pie before he made his temperamental exit."

"I don't blame him," said Hixie. "You were picking on him."

"Why don't you mind your own business and concentrate on stuffing your face, dear? You do it so well!"

"See?" Hixie said, batting her eyelids. "The skinny ones always have miserable dispositions."

"Really!" Rosemary protested in her gentle voice. "Do we have to talk like this in front of Mr. Qwilleran?"

Joy put her face in her hands. "I'm sorry, Jim. My nerves are tied in knots. I've been . . . working too hard. Excuse me." She left the table hurriedly.

The meal ended with stilted scraps of conversation. Hixie talked about the cookbook she was writing. Rosemary extolled the healthful properties of blackstrap molasses. William wondered who had won the ball game in Milwaukee.

After dinner Qwilleran called Arch Riker at home, using the public telephone in the foyer. "I've sure walked into something at Maus Haus," he said, speaking in a low voice. "The tenants are all one big scrappy family, and Joy is definitely upset. She says she's overworked, but it looks like domestic trouble to me. I wish I could get her away for a visit with you and Rosie. It might do her some good."

"Don't take any chances until you know the score," Riker warned him. "If it's marital trouble, she might be using you."

"She wouldn't do that. Poor kid! I still think of her as twenty years old."

"How do you size up her husband?"

"He's a conceited ass."

"Ever meet an artist who wasn't? They all overrate themselves."

"But there's something pitiful about the guy. For all I know, he may have talent. I haven't seen his work. Someone said he was a slob potter, whatever that means."

"It doesn't sound good . . . How about your new column? Are you going to do a story on Maus?"

"If I can pin him down. He's gone to an MSG meeting tonight."

"What's that?"

"Meritorious Society of Gastronomes. A bunch of food snobs."

"Qwill," said Riker in a serious voice, "watch your step, will you? About Joy, I mean."

"I'm no kid, Arch."

"Well, it's spring, you know."

FOUR

WHEN QWILLERAN RETURNED to Number Six, he found Koko and Yum Yum locked in mortal combat with the bearskin rug, which they had chased into a corner. The poor beast, powerless against two determined Siamese, had skidded across the glossy tile floor and was cowering, with back humped and jaws gaping, under the massive carved desk.

Qwilleran was haranguing the cats and dragging the rug back to its rightful position in front of the captain's bed when there was a knock on the door, and—despite a promise he had made to himself—his heart flipped when he saw Joy standing there. Her hair was hanging down to her waist, and she was wearing something filmy and apple green. Although her eyes looked puffed, her composure had returned.

She smiled her funny little smile and peeked into the apartment hesitantly. "Do you have company? I thought I heard you talking to someone."

"Just the cats," Qwilleran said. "When you live

alone, it's sometimes necessary to hear the sound of your own voice, and they're good listeners."

"May I come in? I tried to call you, but your phone isn't connected."

"Mrs. Marron said she'd call the phone company."

"Better do it yourself," Joy said. "There's been a tragedy in her family, and she's still in a daze. Forgets to put potatoes in the potato pancakes. Puts detergent in the soup. She may poison us all before she gets back to normal."

She and her gauzy gown fluttered into the apartment, accompanied by a zephyr of perfume, suggesting cinnamon.

"Look at those beautiful cats!" She gathered Koko in her arms, and he permitted it, much to Qwilleran's surprise and pleasure. Koko was a man's cat and not used to being cuddled. Joy scratched the sensitive zone behind his ears and massaged the top of his head with her chin, while Koko purred, crossed his eyes, and turned his ears inside out.

"Look at him! The old lecher!" Qwilleran said. "I think he likes your green dress . . . So do I!"

"Cats can't distinguish colors," Joy said. "Did you know that? Raku's vet told me." She sighed and hugged Koko tightly, burying her face in the ruff around his neck. "Koko's fur smells like something good to eat."

"That's the aroma of the old house we just moved out of. It always smelled like baked potatoes when the furnace was on. Cats' fur seems to pick up house odors."

"I know. Raku's fur used to smell like wet clay." Joy squeezed her eyes shut and gulped. "He was such a wonderful little friend. It kills me not to know what's happened to him."

"Did you advertise?"

"In both papers. I didn't get a single call—except from one crackpot—some fellow trying to disguise his voice . . . Be sure to keep your cats indoors, won't you?"

"Don't worry about that. I keep them under lock and

key. They mean a lot to me."

Joy looked out the window. The river flowed black between two lighted shorelines, and she shuddered. "I hate water. I was in a boat accident a few years ago, and I still have nightmares of drowning."

"It used to be a beautiful river, they tell me. It's polluted now."

"In our apartment I'm always dropping the blinds to shut out the river, and Dan's always raising them."

Qwilleran took the hint and lowered the Roman shades.

Still carrying Koko over her shoulder, Joy moved about the apartment as if looking for clues to Qwilleran's personal life. She touched his red plaid bathrobe draped over one of the carved Spanish dining chairs. She admired the Mackintosh coat of arms propped on top of the bookcase. She glanced at titles on the shelves. "Have you read all these books? You're such a brain!" At the desk she examined the antique ebony book rack, the ragged dictionary, the typewriter, and the sheet of paper in the machine. "What does this mean? These initials—BW."

"That's Koko's typing. He's ordering his breakfast, I think. Beef Wellington."

Joy laughed—a long, musical trill. "Oh, Jim, you've got a wild imagination."

"It's good to hear your laughter again, Joy."

"It's good to laugh, believe me. I haven't done it for so long . . . Listen! What's the matter with the other cat?"

Yum Yum had retreated to a far corner and was calling in a piteous voice, until Koko jumped from Joy's arms and went to comfort her.

"Jealous," Qwilleran said.

The cats exchanged sympathetic licks. Yum Yum squeezed her eyes shut while Koko passed a long pink tongue over her eyes, nose, and whiskers, and then she returned the compliment.

Joy stopped circling the apartment and draped herself over the arm of the big plaid chair.

"Where's Dan tonight?" Qwilleran inquired.

"Out. As usual! . . . Would you like a tour of the pottery?"

"I don't want to cause trouble. If he doesn't want—"

"He's being ridiculous! Ever since we arrived here, Dan's been mysteriously secretive about our new work. You'd think we were surrounded by spies, trying to steal our ideas!" Joy jumped off the arm of the chair impulsively. "Come on. Our exhibition pots are locked up, and Dan's got the key, but I can show you the clay room and the wheel and the kilns."

They went downstairs to the Great Hall and along the kitchen corridor to the pottery. A heavy steel door opened into a low-ceilinged room filmed with dust. Like a veil, the fine dust covered the floor, worktables, shelves, plaster molds, scrapbooks, broken pots, and rows of crocks with cryptic labels. Dust gave the room a ghostly pallor.

"What's the old suicide mystery connected with this place?" Qwilleran asked.

"An artist was drowned—a long time ago—and some people thought it was murder. Remind me to tell you about it later. I have an interesting new angle on it." She led the way into a large, dismal area that smelled damp and earthy. Everything seemed to be caked with mud. "This is the clay room, and the mechanical equipment is all very old and primitive. That big cylinder is the blunger that mixes the clay. Then it's stored in a tank under the floor and eventually formed into big pancakes on the filter press over there . . . after which it's chewed up by the pug mill and formed into loaves, which are stored in those big bins."

"There must be an easier way," Qwilleran ventured.

"Every step has its purpose. This used to be a big operation fifty years ago. Now we do a few tiles for architects and some garden sculpture for landscape designers—plus our own creative work." Joy walked into a smaller room. "This is our studio. And this is my kick-wheel." She sat on a bench at the clay-coated machine and activated a shaft with a kick-bar, spinning the wheel. "You throw a lump of clay on the wheel and shape it as it spins."

"Looks pretty crude."

"They had wheels of this type in ancient Egypt," Joy said. "We also have a couple of electric wheels, but the kick-wheel is more intimate, I think."

"Did you make that square vase with the blobs of clay on it?"

"No, that's one of Dan's glop pots that your critic didn't like. Wish I could show you my latest, but they're locked up. Maybe it's just as well. Hixie came in here one day and broke a combed pitcher I'd just finished. I could have killed her! She's such a clumsy ox!"

The next room was dry and warm—a large, lofty space with windows just under the ceiling and an Egyptian-style mural running around the top of all four walls. Otherwise, it looked like a bakery. Several ovens stood around the room, and tables held trays of dun-colored tiles, like cookies waiting to be baked.

"These tiles are bone dry and ready for firing," said Joy. "The others are bisque, waiting to be glazed. They'll be used in the chapel that the Pennimans are donating to the university . . . And now you've seen the whole operation. We live in the loft over the clay room. I'd invite you up, only it's a mess. I'm a terrible housekeeper. You should be glad you didn't marry me, Jim." She squeezed Qwilleran's hand. "Shall we have a drink? I've got some bourbon, and we can drink in your apartment, if you don't mind. Is bourbon still your favorite?"

"I'm not drinking. I've signed off the hard stuff," he told her. "But you go and get your bottle, and I'll have a lemon and seltzer with you."

Qwilleran returned to Number Six and found the cats lounging on top of the bookcase. "Well, what do you think of her?" he asked them.

"Yow!" said Koko, squeezing his eyes shut.

When Joy arrived with her bourbon, she said, "You can make yourself very popular in this house by keeping a bottle handy. Mr. Maus doesn't approve of hard liquor—it paralyzes the taste buds—but most of us like to sneak a cocktail now and then."

"How does anyone live here and stay thin?"

"Mr. Maus says a true gourmet never stuffs himself."

Qwilleran poured the drinks. "You were a great cook, Joy. I still remember your homemade raisin bread with honey and lemon frosting."

"Potting is not far removed from baking," she said, curling up comfortably on the built-in bunk. "Wedging clay is like kneading dough. Applying a glaze is like frosting a cake."

"How did you happen to take up potting?"

Joy gazed wistfully into the past. "When I left Chicago so suddenly, Jim, it had nothing to do with you. I adored you—I really did. But I wasn't satisfied with my life . . . and I didn't know what I wanted."

"If you had only explained—"

"I didn't know how. It was easier just to . . . disappear. Besides, I was afraid you'd change my mind."

"Where did you go?"

"San Francisco. I worked in restaurants for a while and then supervised the kitchen on a large ranch. It was operated as a pottery school, and eventually they let me handle some clay. I learned fast, won prizes, and I've been potting ever since."

Qwilleran, relaxing in the big plaid arm chair, took time to light his pipe. "Is that how you met Dan?"

She nodded. "Dan said there was too much competition in California, so we moved to Florida, but I hated that state! I couldn't create. I felt a hundred years old in Florida, so we went back to the Coast until we got the offer to come here."

"No kids?"

Joy took a long, slow sip of her drink. "Dan didn't—that is, he wanted to be free to be poor. And I had my work, which was time-consuming and fulfilling. Did you ever marry, Jim?"

"I gave it a try. I've been divorced for several years."

"Tell me about her."

"She was an advertising woman—very successful."

"But what did she look like?"

"You." Qwilleran allowed himself to look at Joy fondly. "Why are we talking in the past tense? She's still alive—though not well and not happy."

"Are you happy, Jim?"

"I have good days and bad days."

"You look marvelous! You're the type that improves with age. And that mustache makes you look so romantic. Jim—I've never forgotten you—not for a single day." She slid off the bunk and sat on the arm of his chair, leaning toward him and letting her hair fall around them in a thick brown curtain. "You were my first," she whispered, close to his lips.

"And you were my first," he replied softly.

"Yow!" said an imperious voice from the top of the bookcase. A book crashed to the floor. Cats flew in all directions, and the spell was broken.

Joy sat up and sighed deeply. "Forgive me for that silly outburst at dinner tonight. I'm not like that—really I'm not. I'm beginning to hate myself."

"Everyone flies off the handle once in a while."

"Jim," she said abruptly. "I'm going to get a divorce."

"Joy, you shouldn't— I mean, you must think it through carefully. You know how impulsive you are."

"I've been thinking about it for a long time."

"What's the trouble between you and Dan? Or don't you want to talk about it?"

She glanced around the room, as if searching for the words. "I don't know. It's just because . . . well, I'm *me* and he's *himself*. I won't bore you with details. It may be selfish of me, but I know I could do better on my own. He's dragging me down, Jim."

"Is he jealous of your work?" Qwilleran was thinking of the six-hundred-piece table service.

"I'm sure of it, although I try to keep a low profile. Dan has never been really successful. I've had better reviews and bigger sales—and without even trying very hard." Joy hesitated. "No one knows it, but I have fantastic ideas for glazes that I've been holding back. They'd be a sensation, I guarantee."

"Why have you held them back?"

She shrugged. "Trying to play the good wife, trying not to surpass my husband. I know that's old-fashioned. The only way I can shake loose and be honest with myself as an artist is to get out of this marriage. I tell you, Jim, I'm wasting my life! You know how old I am. I'm beginning to want comforts. I'm tired of making my own clothes out of remnants and driving an ancient Renault without a heater . . . Well, it *does* have a heater, but there's this big hole in the floor—"

"You'd better get some legal advice," Qwilleran suggested. "Why don't you discuss it with Maus?"

"I did. His firm doesn't handle divorces—only very dignified corporate stuff—but he referred me to another attorney. And now I'm stymied."

"Why?"

She smiled her pathetic smile. "No money."

"The eternal problem," Qwilleran agreed.

"I had a little money of my own before we were married, but Dan has it tied up somehow. You know I was always bored with financial matters, so I didn't question him about it. Wasn't that dumb? I was too busy making pots. It's an obsession. I can't keep my hands out of clay." She pondered awhile and then added in a low voice, "But I know where I could raise some cash . . . with a little polite blackmail."

"Joy!" Qwilleran exploded. "I hope you're kidding."

"I'd be discreet," she said coolly. "I've found some documents in the attic of the pottery that would embarrass a few people . . . Don't look so horrified, Jim. There's nothing sinister about it—simply a business transaction."

"Don't you dare! You could get into serious trouble." Qwilleran stroked his mustache reflectively. "What, uh . . . how much money would you need?"

"Probably—I don't know—maybe a thousand, to begin with . . . Oh, Jim, I've got to get out of this suffocating situation. Sometimes I just want to jump into that horrid river!"

Joy was still sitting on the arm of his chair, but she was straight-backed and tense now. The lamplight, hitting her face in a certain way, revealed wrinkles around her eyes and mouth. The sight of his childhood sweetheart with signs of age in her face filled Qwilleran with sadness and affection, and after a moment's silence he said, "I could lend you something."

Joy showed genuine surprise. "Would you really, Jim? I don't know what to say. It would save my life! I'd sign a note, of course."

"I don't have much savings," he said. "I've had some rough sledding in recent years, but I won a cash prize at the *Fluxion* in January, and I could let you have—about seven hundred and fifty."

"Oh, Jim! How can I thank you?" She swooped down to kiss him, then jumped up, grabbed Koko from his blue cushion, and whirled around the room with the surprised cat.

Qwilleran went to the desk to write a check, automatically reaching for his glasses, then changing his mind out of sheer vanity.

Joy leaned over his shoulder to watch and gave his temple another kiss, while Koko struggled to get out of her enthusiastic embrace.

"Why don't you pour yourself another drink—for good luck," Qwilleran suggested, fumbling with the checkbook and concealing the figure that represented his meager balance. He was lending this money against his better judgment, and yet he knew he could not have done otherwise.

After Joy had gone back to her own apartment, he deducted the amount of the check and wished he had not bought the new suit or the antique scale. He looked at the note she had signed, written in the absurd hand he remembered so well—all *u*'s and *w*'s.

"I oww Juu Qwwww $750," it read, and it was signed "Jww Gwww." She had never been willing to take time to cross *t*'s and loop *h*'s. Funny, lovable, exhilarating, capricious Joy, Qwilleran thought. What would the future hold for both of them?

The cats had behaved themselves, more or less; that was not always the case when Qwilleran had a woman visiting his living quarters. Koko was a self-appointed chaperon with his own ideas of social decorum.

"Good cat!" said Qwilleran, and in his mood of reckless indulgence he gave them their second dinner. He opened a can of lobster—the last of their Christmas present from the affluent Mary Duckworth. Koko went wild, racing around the apartment and singing in a falsetto interspersed with chesty growls.

"Do you think I did the right thing tonight?" Qwilleran asked him. "It leaves me right back where I was before. Broke!" And the man was so preoccupied with his own wonderment that he failed to notice Koko's sudden silence.

After their feast, the cats went to sleep in the big chair, and Qwilleran spent his first night in the new bed. Lying on his side and staring out of the studio window, he had a full view of the navy-blue sky and a string of lights marking the opposite bank of the river. For several hours sleep evaded him. This time it was not his past that kept him awake but his future.

He heard and identified all the sounds of a new habitat: the hum of traffic on River Road, a lonely boat whistle, a radio or stereo somewhere in the building, and eventually the crunch of tires on the crushed stone of the driveway. He guessed it would be Maus returning from his gourmet meeting, or Max Sorrel coming home from his restaurant, or Dan Graham in the old Renault, returning from some rendezvous. The garage door creaked, and soon there were footsteps tapping on the tiles of the Great Hall. Somewhere a door closed. After that there was the distant rumble of an approaching storm, and occasionally the sky flashed lavender.

Qwilleran had no idea at what hour he fell asleep—or how long he had slept when he was startled awake by a scream. Whether it was the real thing or a fragment of his dream, it was impossible to say. He had been dreaming intensely—a silly dream about mountain climbing. He was standing triumphantly on the summit of a snow-white mountain of mashed potatoes, gazing across a sea of brown gravy. Someone shouted a warning, and there was a scream, and he waked.

He raised his head and listened sharply. Silence. The scream, Qwilleran decided, had been part of the sound effects of his dream. He switched on the bed lamp to check the time, and that was when he noticed the cats. They had raised their heads and were listening, too. Their ears were pointed forward. Both heads rotated slowly as they scanned the soundscape in every direction. The cats had heard something. It had not been a dream.

Still, the man told himself, it could have been squealing tires on River Road, or the garage door creaking again. Noises magnified themselves on the threshold of waking. At that moment he heard the sound of creaking hinges quite plainly, followed by the rumble of a car engine, and he jumped out of bed in time to see a light-colored convertible pulling away from the building. He glanced at his watch. It was three twenty-five.

The cats laid their ears back and their chins on their paws and settled down to sleep, and Qwilleran closed the ventilating panes in the big studio window as the first drops of rain splashed on the glass like enormous tears.

FIVE

WHEN QWILLERAN AWOKE Wednesday morning, it took him a few seconds to get his bearings in the strange apartment. He looked at the sky through the studio window—a vast panorama of blue, broken only by a single soaring pigeon. He stared up at the beamed ceiling two stories overhead, noted the big plaid chair, remembered the white bearskin rug. Then the events of the previous day came rushing into his mind: his new home in a pottery . . . the nearness of Joy after all the years of separation . . . her marital trouble . . . the $750 loan . . . and the sound he had heard in the night. In daylight the recollection of it seemed considerably less alarming. He stretched and yawned, disturbing Yum Yum, who was huddled in his armpit, and then he heard a bell ring. Koko was standing on the desk with one paw on the typewriter.

"Coming right up!" Qwilleran said, hoisting himself out of bed. He put on his red plaid bathrobe and went to the tiny kitchen to open a can of food for the cats. "I know you ordered beef Wellington," he told Koko, "but you'll have to settle for red salmon. This is two dollars a can. *Bon appétit*!"

The prospect of breakfast touched off a joyous scuffle. Yum Yum kicked Koko with her hind leg like a mule, and he gave her a push. They went into a clinch, pummeling each other until Koko played too rough. Then Yum Yum sprang back and started to circle, lashing her tail. Suddenly she pounced and grabbed him by the throat, but Koko got a hug-hold, and they rolled over and over, locked together. By secret signal both cats quit the fight at the same instant and licked each other's imaginary wounds.

When Qwilleran dressed and went downstairs, he followed the aroma of bacon and coffee into the kitchen. At the big round table Robert Maus was solemnly breakfasting on croissants and marmalade and French chocolate, while Hixie waited for Mrs. Marron to make French toast.

Qwilleran helped himself to orange juice. "Where's everybody this morning?"

"Max never gets up for breakfast," Hixie reported promptly, as she spooned sour cream into her coffee. "William's gone to an early class. Rosemary always has wheat germ in her apartment. Charlotte came early and had 'a bite to eat' big enough to choke a horse, and now she's gone to the Red Cross to roll bandages, or whatever she does there on Wednesday mornings."

"Miss Roop," Maus explained in his pedantic manner, "devotes a generous amount of time to . . . volunteer clerical work at the blood bank, for which she must be . . . admired."

"Do you suppose she's atoning for something wicked in her past?" Hixie asked.

The attorney turned to her in solemn disapproval. "You are, to all appearances, a nasty young lady. Furthermore, I find the use of . . . *sour cream* in coffee an extremely . . . revolting habit."

"Hurry up with the toast, Marron baby," said Hixie. "I'm starving."

"Do the Grahams come down to breakfast?" Qwilleran asked.

"They haven't shown up this morning." She was heaping gooseberry jam on a crusty French roll. "I wish I had a job like theirs, so I could be my own boss and set my own hours."

"My dear young woman," Maus told her gravely, "you would be bankrupt within six months. You are entirely without . . . self-discipline." Then he turned to Qwilleran. "I trust you are sufficiently . . . comfortable in Number Six?"

As he spoke, Qwilleran noticed for the first time a slight discoloration around the attorney's left eye. "Everything's fine," the newsman said, after a barely perceptible pause, "but I heard something strange in the night. Did anyone else hear an outcry about three-thirty this morning? It sounded like a woman's scream."

There was no reply at the table. Hixie opened her eyes wide and shook her head. Maus calmly went on chewing with the kind of concentration he always gave to the process.

It was characteristic of members of the legal profession never to show surprise, Qwilleran reminded himself. "Maybe it was the garage door that I heard," he suggested.

Maus said, "Mrs. Marron, kindly ask William to . . . lubricate the garage doors when he returns."

"By the way," said the newsman, pouring himself a cup of the excellent coffee, "I'd like to write a column on your cooking philosophy, Mr. Maus, if you're agreeable." He waited patiently for the attorney's response.

After a while it came, accompanied by a gracious nod. "I cannot, at this time, see any . . . objection."

"Perhaps you could have dinner with me tonight at the Toledo Tombs—as the guest of the *Daily Fluxion*."

At the mention of the epicurean restaurant Maus brightened noticeably. "By all means! We shall have their . . . eels in green sauce. They also prepare a superb veal dish with tarragon and Japanese mushrooms. You must allow me to order."

They set a time and place to meet, and Maus left for his office, carrying an attaché case. Qwilleran had seen Mrs. Marron stock it with some small cartons, a thermos bottle, and a cold artichoke. Hixie left soon afterward, having finished a plate of bacon and French toast, swimming in melted butter and maple syrup and sprinkled with chopped pecans. Qwilleran remained alone, wondering about his landlord's black eye.

When Mrs. Marron came to the table to remove the plates, she said, "You should eat something, Mr. Qwilleran—something to stick to the ribs."

"There's too much sticking to my ribs already."

The housekeeper lingered at the table, slowly piling dishes on a tray and slowly rearranging them. "Mr. Qwilleran," she said, "I heard something last night, and it wasn't the garage door."

"What time did you hear it?"

"It was after three o'clock. I know that much. My room is in the back, and I don't sleep very good lately, so I watch television in bed. I use the earphone, so I don't disturb anybody."

"Exactly what did you hear?"

"I thought it was tomcats scrapping down at the boat docks, but it could've been somebody screaming."

"I hope everyone in the house is all right," Qwilleran said. "Why don't you check on Mrs. Whiting and the Grahams?"

"Do you think I should?"

"Under the circumstances, Mrs. Marron, I think it would be advisable."

I'm beginning to sound like Robert Maus, he told himself as he sipped black coffee and waited for the housekeeper's return.

"Mrs. Whiting is all right; she's doing her exercises," Mrs. Marron reported. "But I couldn't get ahold of the Grahams. The door to the pottery is locked. I knocked three, four times, but nobody answered. If they're upstairs in their apartment, they can't hear."

"You don't have a key to the pottery?" He glanced at

a key rack on the kitchen wall.

The housekeeper shook her head. "Those are only the apartment keys, so I can clean. Shall I go around the backyard and up the fire escape?"

"Let's try telephoning," Qwilleran suggested. "Do you know the Grahams' number?"

"What shall I say to them?"

"I'll do the talking."

Mrs. Marron dialed a number on the kitchen phone and handed the receiver to Qwilleran. A man's voice answered.

"Mr. Graham? Good morning! This is Jim Qwilleran, your new neighbor. Is everything under control at your end of the building? We thought we smelled smoke . . . That's good. Just playing safe. By the way, you're missing a fine breakfast. Mrs. Marron is making French toast . . . Can't tempt you? Too bad. I really wanted to discuss the pottery operation. The *Fluxion* might run a feature story to tie in with your exhibition . . . You will? Good! I'll wait."

"Smoke?" said Mrs. Marron when Qwilleran had handed back the receiver. "I didn't smell any smoke."

A few minutes later Dan Graham walked into the kitchen, looking thinner and more forlorn than ever. He dropped gracelessly into a chair and said he would have coffee and a roll, that's all.

Mrs. Marron said, "I can make some of those cornmeal johnnycakes you like."

"Just a roll."

"Or a stack of wheatcakes. It will only take a minute."

The potter scowled at her, and she went back to the sink and started stacking plates in the dishwasher.

Qwilleran resisted an impulse to ask the man about his wife. Instead he hinted at vast possibilities for free publicity, and Dan warmed up.

"The newspapers ought to print more articles like that," he said, "instead of tearing us down all the time. Hell, they don't pan the new model cars or those stupid clothes they design in Paris. Why do they pick on artists? The papers hire some nincompoop as a critic and let him air his private beefs and chase people away from the exhibitions. A lot of people would like contemporary art if the local newspapers didn't keep telling them how bad it is. They should be explaining to the public how to appreciate what they see."

"I'll speak to our feature editor," Qwilleran said. "It's not my beat and I can't make the decision, but I'm sure Arch Riker will send a photographer over here. He'll probably want to take some shots of you and your wife, as well as your new pottery. A good human interest story might make a spread in the Sunday supplement. In color!"

Dan hung his head and looked deep into his coffee cup. "There's the hitch," he said finally. "I know you fellows on the paper like cheesecake and all that kind of stuff, but you'll have to settle for a broken-down he-potter with freckles." He said it with a twisted smile.

"Why? Doesn't Mrs. Graham like to be photographed? She's very attractive."

Dan glanced toward the sink, where Mrs. Marron was peeling apples, and lowered his voice. "The old girl's cleared out."

"She's what? She's left you?" Qwilleran had not expected anything to happen so soon, and yet he should have known that Joy would fly into action.

"Yes, she's decamped—vamoosed—flown the coop, if you know what I mean. It's not the first time, either." Again there was the brave one-sided smile, and Qwilleran realized—partly with pity and partly with scorn—that the grimace was an unconscious imitation of Joy's appealing mannerism.

"Once when we were in Florida," the potter went on, "she ran off. No explanation, no note, no nothing. She really left me standing on my ear that time, but she came back, and everything straightened out. Women don't know what they want . . . So I'll just sit tight like a bug in a rug and wait for her to have her fling and get over what's eating her. She'll be back, don't worry. Too bad she had to go right before the exhibition, that's all."

Qwilleran, who was seldom at a loss for words, hardly knew what to say. It was obvious he knew more than the husband about Joy's intentions. "When did you first realize she'd gone?" he asked, trying to appear sympathetic but not personally involved.

"Woke up this morning and couldn't find hide nor hair of the woman! Might as well tell you that we had a little argument last night, but I didn't think it was anything serious." Dan stroked his unshaven jaw thoughtfully and looked hurt and dejected.

Qwilleran noticed that the potter's right thumb was missing up to the first joint, and for a moment his loyalties were divided. A hand injury would be the worst thing that could happen to a potter; was that the reason for his declining success? He could also sympathize with a husband deserted by an ambitious wife; he had gone through the same humiliating experience.

"Did she take the car?" Qwilleran asked.

"No, she left it here. I'd be in a fix if she'd run off with the old jalopy. It's not much, but it gets me there and back."

"Then what did she use for transportation in the middle of the night?"

Dan's mouth fell open. "The bus, I reckon. They run up and down River Road all night."

Or, thought Qwilleran, did she drive away with the owner of the light-colored convertible at three in the morning? . . . Then the dismal possibility flashed into his mind. It could be that his $750 had financed Joy's elopement with another man.

No! He refused to believe that! Still, his face felt hot and cold by turns, and he ran a hand over his forehead. Was he an accomplice or a victim, or both? He was a fool, he decided, either way. His first impulse was to stop payment on the check. As a newsman and a professional cynic he suspected he had been duped, but a better instinct told him to have faith in Joy—if he loved her, and he privately admitted it now: He had never really stopped loving Joy Wheatley.

I know Joy, he told himself. No matter how desperate she was, she would never do that to *me*. Then he remembered the scream.

"I don't want to alarm you, Dan," he said in a calm voice that belied his confusion, "but are you sure she left the premises voluntarily?"

Dan, who had been staring gloomily into his coffee cup, looked up sharply. "How do you mean?"

"I mean . . . I thought I heard a woman scream last night, and shortly after that, I heard a car drive away."

The potter gave a short, bitter laugh. "Did you hear that ruckus? Crazy woman! Tell you what happened. When I came home last night, it was sort of late. I know these guys downtown—all artists, more or less—we play poker, drink a few beers. Well, it was sort of late, and Joy was sitting up waiting. Miffed, I guess. There she was—sitting at the wheel and throwing a pot and looking daggers at me when I came in. And you know what? She was working at the wheel with her hair hanging down a mile! I've warned her about that, but she's cocky and never pays any attention to what I say."

Dan brooded over the situation, staring into his empty coffee cup until Qwilleran poured a refill and said, "Well, what happened?"

"Oh, we had the usual scrap about this and that, and she started tossing her head around—the way she does when she gets on her high horse. And then—dammit if she didn't get her hair caught in the wheel, just as I was afraid. Could've scalped her! Could've broken her neck if I hadn't been there to throw the switch and stop the thing. Crazy woman!"

"And you say she screamed?"

"Woke up the whole house, probably. I tell you it gave me a holy scare, too. I don't know what I'd do if anything happened to that old girl."

Qwilleran wore a frown that passed for sympathy, although it stemmed from his own dilemma.

"I'm not worried. She'll be back," Dan said. He pushed his chair away from the table and stood up, stretching and patting his diaphragm. "Gotta get to work now. Gotta start setting up the exhibition. See if you can do anything for me at the paper, will you?" He reached in his hip pocket and found his wallet, from which he carefully withdrew a folded clipping. He handed it to Qwilleran with poorly concealed pride. "Here's what the top-drawer critic in L.A. said about my one-man show. This guy really knew his onions, I'm not kidding."

It was a very old clipping, the newsprint yellow and disintegrating where it had been folded.

After Dan had left, patting the rear pocket where he had stowed the wallet and the worn clipping, Qwilleran asked the housekeeper, "Who drives a light-colored convertible around here?"

"Mr. Sorrel has a light car. Kind of—baby blue," she added with a catch in her voice.

"Have you seen him this morning?"

"No, he never gets up early. He works late every night."

"I think I'll take a stroll around the grounds," Qwilleran told her. "I want to put my cat on a leash and give him a little exercise. And if you'll tell me where to find the oilcan, I'll fix that garage door."

"You don't have to do that, Mr. Qwilleran. William is supposed to—"

"No trouble, Mrs. Marron. I'll oil the hinges, and William can cut the grass. It needs it."

"If you walk down to the river," she said in a shaking voice, "be careful of the boardwalk. There might be some loose boards."

Back in his apartment Qwilleran found the cats bedded down for their morning nap on the bunk, their legs and tails interwoven to make a single brown fur mat between them. He lifted the sleeping Koko, whose body had the limp weight of a sack of flour, and coaxed his yawning head through the collar of a blue leather harness. Then, using a piece of nylon cord as a leash, he led the reluctant cat out the door—still yawning, stretching and staggering.

They circled the balcony before going downstairs. Qwilleran wanted to read the nameplates on the doors. Adjoining his own was Rosemary Whiting's apartment from which he could hear the sound of music—then that of Max Sorrel, where guttural snoring could be heard behind the closed door. On the opposite side of the balcony were the nameplates of Hixie Rice, Charlotte Roop, and Robert Maus. Why nameplates? Qwilleran started to wonder, but he dropped the question; there were too many other things on his mind.

He led Koko down the stairs, across the slick brown tiles of the Great Hall, and out into the side yard of Maus Haus. For Koko, an apartment dweller all his life, grass was a rare treat. On the lawn, still wet from the night's rain, he tried to inspect each blade personally, rejecting one and snapping his jaws on the next, with a selectivity understood only by his species. After each moist step through the grass he shook his paws fastidiously.

There was an open carport on the east side of the building, obviously a new addition. It sheltered a dark blue compact and an old dust-colored Renault. The latter did indeed have a hole in the floor, large enough for a size 12 shoe, the newsman estimated.

From there a gravel path led down to the river, where two weathered benches stood on a rotting boardwalk. The water—brown as gravy in daylight and with an indefinable stench—riffled sluggishly against the old piling.

Koko did not care for it. He wanted nothing to do with the river. He pulled away from the boardwalk and stayed on the wet grass until they started back up the path. Once he stopped to sniff a bright blue-green object on the edge of the gravel, and Qwilleran picked it up—a small glazed ceramic piece the size and shape of a beetle. Scratched on the underside were the initials J.G.

He dropped it in his pocket, tugged on the leash, and led Koko back toward the house.

From the rear, the misshapen building looked like a grotesque bird with a topknot of chimneys, its carport and garage like awkward wings, its fire escapes and ledges like ruffled feathers. For eyes there were the two large staring windows of the Grahams' loft, and as Qwilleran looked up at them, he saw a figure inside move hastily away.

Coming to the three-stall garage, he opened the lift-doors. Only one of them creaked, and only one of the stalls was occupied. The car was a light blue convertible. Closing the garage door, Qwilleran examined the car carefully, inside and out—the floor, the upholstery, the instrument panel. It was very clean.

"What about this, Koko?" he muttered. "It's almost too clean."

Koko was busy sniffing oil stains on the concrete floor.

When the two returned to Number Six, Koko allowed Yum Yum to wash his face and ears, and Qwilleran paced the floor, wondering where Joy had gone, whether she had gone alone, when (if ever) she would get in touch with him, and whether he would ever see his money again. He had been unemployed for so long, before being hired by the *Daily Fluxion*, that $750 was a small fortune.

He wondered if Kipper & Fine had started alterations on his new suit, and he was tempted to call them and cancel the order. Today he felt no desire for a new suit. It had been a short spring. And now—added to his mental discomforts—he realized that he was desperately hungry.

There was a sudden disturbance on the desk—a shuffling of papers, a clicking of typewriter keys, some skidding of pencils and pens, and then a light clatter as Qwilleran's new reading glasses fell to the floor.

Qwilleran sprang to the desk as Koko made a headlong dive into the big chair. "Bad cat!" the man shouted at him. Fortunately the glasses had been saved by their heavy frames. But Qwilleran felt a tremor in the roots of his mustache when he noticed the sheet of paper in the typewriter. He put on his glasses and looked more closely.

Koko had discovered the top row of keys. He had put one paw on the numeral three and the other on zero.

SIX

SHORTLY AFTER NOON Qwilleran hurried into the Press Club and joined Arch Riker at a table for two, where the feature editor was passing the time with a martini.

"Sorry to be late," Qwilleran said. "I had to rush Koko to the vet."

"What's wrong?"

"I had him out in the backyard at Maus Haus, and he ate a lot of grass. When we got back to the apartment, he threw up, and I thought he'd eaten something poisonous."

"All cats eat grass and throw up," said Riker. "That's how they get rid of hair balls."

"Now I know. They told me at the pet hospital. But I wasn't taking any chances. Too bad he had to select my new shoes as a receptacle. *Both* shoes!"

"You should brush the cats. The kids brush ours every day, and we never have any trouble."

"Why don't people tell me these things? I just paid fifteen dollars for an office call." Qwilleran lighted a pipeful of tobacco and signaled the waitress for coffee.

"Well, what's the big news you mentioned on the phone?" Riker asked.

Qwilleran puffed his pipe intently and took his time about answering. "History repeats itself. Joy has disappeared—again."

"You're kidding!"

"I'm not kidding."

"So she's up to her old tricks."

"I don't know what to believe," Qwilleran said. He told Riker about Joy's visit to his apartment and her plans for a divorce, but not about the $750 check.

Riker said: "Rosie was going to call her up and invite her over for some girl talk. She thought it might help."

"Too late now."

"What does her husband say about it?"

"He says she's done it before. He says she always comes back. But he doesn't know what I know."

"What does he look like, anyway? Rosie told me to find out. You know how women are."

"He looks and talks like a hayseed. Not Joy's type at all. Tall and gangling. Washed-out red hair and freckles. Talks like a hayseed, too. He thinks he's got such a colorful vocabulary, but his clichés are pathetic, and his slang is out of date by about thirty years. If you ask me, he's a guy who wants desperately to be somebody and never will."

"The man who loses the girl never thinks highly of the winner, I might point out," said Riker, looking smug and enjoying his own trenchant observation.

"Joy said it herself. She said he's no crashing success as a potter."

"Why would a classy girl like Joy pick someone like that?"

"Who knows? She always liked tall men. Maybe he's a great lover. Maybe his freckles appealed to her maternal instinct."

Riker ordered another martini, and Qwilleran went on: "Now that you've had a drink, I'll tell you the rest of the story. I lent Joy some money just before she vanished."

The editor choked on an olive. "Oh, no! How much?"

"Seven-fifty."

"Seven *hundred* and fifty? Your prize money?"

Qwilleran nodded sheepishly.

"What a pushover! Cash?"

"I wrote a check."

"Stop payment, Qwill."

"She may need it—badly—wherever she is. On the other hand," he said reluctantly, "she may have run off with another guy. Or . . . something may have happened to her."

"Like what? Where did you get that idea?" Riker was familiar with Qwilleran's hunches; they were always totally correct—or totally unfounded.

"Last night I heard a scream—a woman's scream—and shortly afterward a car pulled out of the garage." He tamped his mustache nervously.

Riker recognized the gesture. It meant that his friend was on the scent of another misdeed, great or small, real or imagined. Qwilleran's early years on the police beat had given him a sixth sense about crime. What Riker did not know—and would not have believed—was the unique sensitivity in that oversized mustache. Qwilleran's hunches were usually accompanied by a prickling sensation on the upper lip, and when this happened he was never wrong.

Riker said, "Got any theories?"

Qwilleran shook his head. He said nothing about the numbers that Koko had typed, although the recollection made his hair stand on end. "I told Dan about hearing the scream, and he had an explanation. He said Joy got her long hair caught in the wheel."

"What wheel?"

"The potter's wheel. They use it to throw pots. Dan says she screamed and he came to the rescue. I don't know whether to believe it or not."

"I think you're worrying without any cause. She's probably on her way to Chicago to see her aunt, if the old lady's still living."

Qwilleran persisted. "At dinner last night Joy was snapping at everyone. There was something in the air."

"Who else lives in that weird establishment?"

"There's Robert Maus, the lawyer, who owns the place. He can't make a statement on any subject, including the weather, without first considering the pros, cons, legal implications, and tax advantages. Very dignified gent. But here's a curious development: This morning he was nursing a black eye . . . Then there's Max Sorrel, who owns the Golden Lamb Chop. He comes on strong as a ladies' man, and it was his car that drove out of the garage shortly after I heard the scream."

"But you aren't positive he was in it," Riker said. "Joy may have been driving."

"If she was, she gave the car a pat on the rump and sent it home again; it was back in the garage this morning. Dan said she probably went on the River Road bus. If so, she picked a fine time; it was pouring rain."

"Who else lives there?"

"Three women. And a houseboy who's nosy but likable. And a housekeeper." Qwilleran leaned his elbows on the table and massaged his mustache. He remembered Joy's remark about a "discreet" extortion scheme and decided not to mention it.

Riker said, "You're letting your imagination run away with you, Qwill. Nothing's happened to Joy. You wait and see."

"I wish I could believe it."

"Well, anyway, I've got to eat and get back to the office. A syndicate salesman's coming in with some comic strips at two o'clock." He hailed a waitress. "Bowl of bean soup, meatballs and noodles, salad with Roquefort, and let's have some more butter at this table."

"And what'll you have, Skinny?" she asked Qwilleran. "You want cottage cheese again?"

"I'm starving. Quips are not appreciated."

"You want a cheeseburger with french fries? Macaroni and cheese? Ham and sweets?"

"No, I'll take a poached egg," he decided with firm resolve, "and all the celery they've got in the kitchen. I can burn up more calories chewing celery than I get from eating the damn stuff."

"Where are you eating tonight?" Riker asked.

"I've invited Maus to go with me to the Toledo Tombs, and it's going to be a heroic test of willpower on my part. I hear the food's the best in town."

"That's the place where you get a fresh napkin every five minutes. Rosie and I went there for our anniversary, and the waiters made me nervous. After they brought the seventeenth clean ashtray, I started flicking my ashes on the floor under the table."

That afternoon Qwilleran went to the public library to get a book on French food. He also picked up a book on the art of ceramics, without knowing exactly why. At the liquor store he bought a bottle of sherry and some bourbon in preparation for possible visitors to his apartment. He bought a brush at the pet shop. Finally he stopped at a supermarket to buy food for the cats. Goaded by his own unsatisfied appetite and his financial setback, he was hardly in a generous mood.

They're spoiled brats, he told himself. Lobster—red salmon—boned chicken! Other cats eat cat food, and it's about time they faced reality.

He bought a can of Kitty Delight (on sale), some Pussy Pâté (two for the price of one), and a jumbo-size box of Fishy Fritters (with a free offer on the back).

When he arrived home, Koko and Yum Yum were sitting in compact bundles on the windowsill, and their behavior indicated that they sensed the nature of the situation. Instead of chirping and crowing a welcome, they sat motionless and gazed through Qwilleran as if he were invisible.

"Soup's on!" he announced, after smearing a dime's worth of Pussy Pâté on a plate and placing it on the floor.

Neither of the cats moved a whisker.

"Try it! The label says it's delicious."

They seemed totally deaf. There was not even the flicker of an ear. Qwilleran picked Koko up bodily and plumped him down in front of the pâté, and Koko stood there with legs splayed, frozen in the position in which he had landed, glaring at the evil-looking purple smear on the plate. Then he shuddered exquisitely and walked away.

Later that evening Qwilleran described the incident to Robert Maus. "I'm convinced they can read price tags," he said, "but they'll eat the stuff if they get hungry enough."

Maus deliberated a few seconds. "A béarnaise sauce might make it more palatable," he suggested, "or a sprinkling of freshly grated Romano."

The two men had met in the lobby of a downtown building, where an elevator descended to unknown depths and deposited them in a cellar. The subterranean restaurant consisted of a series of cavernous rooms, long and narrow, vaulted in somber black masonry. It had been a sewer before the city installed the new disposal system.

The attorney was greeted with deference, and the two men were conducted to a table resplendent with white napery. Seven wine glasses and fourteen pieces of flat silver glittered at each place. Two waiters draped napkins, lightly scented with orange flower water, across the guests' knees. A captain presented menus bound in gold-tooled Florentine leather, and three busboys officiated at the filling of two water glasses.

Maus waved the chlorinated product away with an imperious gesture. "We drink only bottled water," he said, "and we wish to consult the sommelier."

The wine steward arrived, wearing chains and keys and a properly pompous air, and Maus selected a champagne. Then the two diners perused the menu, which was only slightly smaller than the Sunday edition of the *Fluxion*, offering everything from aquavit to zabaglione, and from avocado suprême rémoulade to zucchini sauté avec hollandaise.

"I might note, in passing," said the attorney sadly, "that the late Mrs. Maus inevitably ordered chopped sirloin when we dined here."

Qwilleran had not realized that Maus was widowed. "Didn't your wife share your interest in *haute cuisine*?"

After some studied breathing Maus replied: "Not that I can, with any good conscience, admit. She once used my best omelet pan for, I regret to say, liver and onions."

Qwilleran clucked his sympathy.

"I suggest we start, if it meets with your approval, Mr. Qwilleran, with the 'French bunion soup,' as it was called in our ménage. Mrs. Maus, as it happened, was a chiropodist by profession, and she had the . . . unfortunate habit of discussing her practice at the dinner table."

Onion soup was served, crusted with melted cheese, and Qwilleran manfully limited himself to three sips. "How did you happen to buy the pottery?" he inquired.

Maus considered his answer carefully. "It was an inheritance," he said at length. "The building was a bequest from my wife's uncle, Hugh Penniman, a patron of the arts and collector of ceramics in particular, who conceived the building as an art center . . . in which capacity it functioned—at great expense to the philanthropist himself—until his death . . . after which it passed to his two sons, who declined the bequest, considering it a white elephant (under the terms imposed by the will) . . . whereupon it fell to my wife and subsequently to me."

"What were the terms of the will?"

"The old gentlemen stipulated that the building must continue to serve the arts, as it were—a proviso synonymous with economic folly in the opinion of my wife's cousins, and not without reason, artists being largely insolvent, as you must be aware. However, I devised the . . . not uninspired expedient of renting the studios to gourmets (since gastronomy is viewed, in the eyes of its practitioners, as an art). At the same time I chose to . . . reactivate the pottery operation, which—I surmised—would prove to be a financial liability with favorable tax consequences, if you follow me."

This recital of facts was terminated by the arrival of the eels in green sauce.

"I've been hearing about a drowning scandal in connection with the pottery," Qwilleran remarked. "When did it happen?"

The attorney drew a slow breath of exasperation. "That unhappy incident is, I assure you, ancient history. Yet time and time again *your newspaper*—a publication for which I entertain only limited admiration, if you will pardon my candor—*your newspaper* disinters the episode and publishes unsavory headlines designed, one can only infer, to titillate a readership of less than average intellect. Now that the building has fallen under my aegis, it is to be hoped there will be no further publicity on the subject. If you are in a position to exert any influence to this end, I shall be indeed . . . grateful."

"By the way," Qwilleran said, "I don't think you should lock the door between the pottery and the apartments. The fire marshal would take a dim view of that."

"The fire door has not, to my knowledge, been locked at any time."

"It was locked this morning—from the inside."

Maus, intent on savoring a morsel of eel, made no reply.

"Is Graham considered a good potter?" Qwilleran asked.

"He is, I am inclined to believe, an excellent technician, with a thorough knowledge of materials, equipment, and the operation of a pottery. The creative talent belongs chiefly, it appears to me, on the distaff side of the family."

"You may not have heard the news," Qwilleran said, "but Mrs. Graham has left her husband. I believe she consulted you about getting a divorce. Well, last night—in the small hours—she cleared out."

Maus continued chewing thoughtfully and then said, "Unfortunate, to say the least."

Qwilleran searched the attorney's face for some revealing reaction but saw only an imperturbable countenance and preoccupied eyes, one of them ringed with a bruise, now turning purple.

The distinguished epicure was engrossed in evaluating the green sauce. He said, "The parsley, it is safe to say, was added a trifle too soon . . . although, as you must know, much controversy can be generated on the subject of herbs. At the Meritorious Society of Gastronomes last evening we enjoyed a stimulating symposium on oregano. The discussion, it eventuated, grew quite . . . stormy."

"Is that how you got that mouse?" Qwilleran asked.

The attorney tenderly touched his left eye. "In the heat of argument, I regret to report, one of our members—an impetuous individual—thrust his fist in my direction at an inopportune time."

The main course and a bottle of white wine were now served in a flurry of excitement by seven members of the restaurant staff. Maus tasted the wine and sent it back, complained about a cigar at the next table, and detected a *soupçon* too much tarragon in the sauce.

Qwilleran viewed with mounting hunger the dish of veal and mushrooms, aswim in delicate juices. He determined, however, to adhere to his regimen: three bites and quit. After the first bite he said to Maus, "Do you think Max Sorrel would make a good personality story for my column?"

The attorney sagely nodded approval. "His restaurant is experiencing certain—shall we say?—difficulties at this time, and it is undoubtedly true that some manner of . . . favorable comment in the press would not go unappreciated. I deem it inadvisable to elucidate, but Mr. Sorrel, I am sure, will be happy to discuss the matter with you, if you so . . . desire."

"And what about Charlotte Roop?"

Maus laid down his knife and fork, which he was manipulating in the European manner. "Ah, there is a jewel! Do not allow yourself to be misled by the fluttering spinster facade. Miss Roop is a successful career woman with remarkable executive ability and integrity of the highest order. If she suffers from certain character defects, it behooves us to leave them unmentioned."

Qwilleran took his second bite. "Rosemary Whiting seems to be very nice. A perfect lady."

"A Canadian," Maus said. His face was beatific as he savored the veal, having come to terms with the excess of tarragon.

"What's her special interest in food?"

"Mrs. Whiting, it pains me to say, is a purveyor of health foods. You may have heard her panegyrics to soybeans and sunflower seeds."

"And Hixie Rice, I understand, is a food writer."

Maus raised his hands in a dignified gesture of resignation. "The young lady writes, in the course of duty, those appalling menus for third-rate restaurants: 'Today's special—a delectable ragout blending tender tidbits of succulent baby lamb with garden-sweet carrots, pristine cubes of choice Michigan potato, and jewellike peas—all in a tasty sauce redolent of the Far East.' That effusion of baroque prose indicates, as you may be aware, yesterday's leftovers drowning in canned gravy . . . with sufficient curry powder to camouflage the rancidity."

Qwilleran took his third bite. "William is an interesting character, too."

"He prattles to excess, alas, and boasts no useful skills, but he is congenial, and his bridge game is not without merit."

The captain and the waiters had been observing, with increasing alarm, Qwilleran's dilatory attitude toward the food, and now there was a stir among the staff as the head chef came storming from the kitchen.

He walked directly toward Qwilleran and demanded, "You no like my cooking?"

"A true gourmet never stuffs himself," the newsman replied calmly. "The food is excellent, rest assured. I'd like to take the rest of this veal home to my cats."

"*Gatti*! Santa Maria! So now I cook for *gatti*!" The chef threw up his hands and charged back to the kitchen.

After the braised fennel amandine and the tossed salad with nasturtium seeds, and the chestnut puree in meringue nests, and the demitasse, Qwilleran reached in his pocket for his pipe and drew forth the turquoise beetle that Koko had found near the waterfront. "Ever see that before?"

Maus nodded. "Mrs. Graham had the charm to present to each of us a scarab—as a token, so to speak, of good fortune. Mine has, unhappily, disappeared—an omen that bodes no good, one would imagine."

Qwilleran paid the check, thankful that the *Fluxion* was footing the bill; he could have lived for a week on the tip alone. And now he was eager to go home. He had made no notes during the dinner interview, as Maus expounded his culinary tenets. The newsman knew that cautious subjects speak more freely when their words are not being recorded. But he had accumulated plenty of material for a column on Robert Maus, and now it was necessary to collect the piquant quotes from the corners of his mind and get them down on paper before they faded from memory. As soon as the waiters brought the cats' veal to the table, wrapped in a linen napkin, the two men departed—Maus radiating gustatory satisfaction and Qwilleran feeling vaguely hungry and a trifle sorry for himself.

When they arrived at Maus Haus, the attorney took his attaché case to the kitchen and Qwilleran climbed the grand staircase, but at the landing he turned right instead of left. A sudden impulse led him to Hixie's apartment.

Just as he raised his hand to knock on the door, he heard a man's voice, and he hesitated. Through the thick oak panel he could hear only the rumble of the masculine voice without distinguishing the words, but the inflections indicated that the man was coaxing and gently arguing. At first it sounded like television drama, but then Qwilleran recognized the second voice in the dialogue.

Hixie was saying, "No! That's final! . . . Thanks a lot but no thanks!" The high pitch of her voice made the words distinguishable.

There was a wheedling reply from the man.

"That doesn't make any difference. You know my terms." She lowered her voice in answer to a question. "Of course I do, but you shouldn't have come here. We agreed you'd never come here . . . All right, just one drink, and then you've got to leave."

Qwilleran knocked on the door.

There was an abrupt silence and a long wait before Hixie's heels could be heard clicking on the floor and approaching the door. "Who is it?" She opened the door cautiously. "Oh, it's you!" she said with a nervous smile. "I was on the telephone. Sorry to keep you waiting." She did not invite him in.

"I just wondered if you'd like to go to a cheese-tasting tomorrow afternoon. It's a press party."

"Yes, I'd love it. Where shall I meet you?"

"How about the lobby of the Stilton Hotel?"

"That's fine. You know me! I love to eat."

"There'll be drinks, of course."

"Love to drink, too." She batted her long false eyelashes.

Qwilleran tried to glance over her shoulder, but the door was only partially open, and the room was in shadow. He saw only a flutter of movement—a bird hopping about in a cage. "See you tomorrow," he said.

Qwilleran preferred to date women with figures more svelte and clothes more tasteful, but he wanted to ask questions, and he was sure that Hixie liked to babble answers. As he walked around the balcony to Number Six, he was determined to keep an ear tuned for activity across the hall. After "just one drink," who would slip out of Hixie's apartment and where would he go? Why, he asked himself, am I such a nosy bastard? But when he unlocked his own door and stepped into the apartment, he forgot his curiosity. The place was a scene of havoc.

All the pictures on the wall over the bookcase were hanging askew. Several books were on the floor with covers spread and pages rumpled. The wastebasket had been overturned, and its contents were strewn about the tile floor. Cushions had been thrown on the floor, and the desktop was swept clean of all but the typewriter. Burglary? Vandalism? Qwilleran glanced swiftly about him before he took a further step into the room. His foot came down on a small object that crunched and pulverized. He stepped quickly aside. Crunch! There were scores of small brown balls scattered about the floor, and the bearskin rug was missing . . . No, it was huddled under the desk.

"You devils!" Qwilleran bellowed. Those brown balls were Fishy Fritters! The open carton lay on the kitchen floor, empty, and beside it was the plate on which the untouched Pussy Pâté had dried to a nauseating crust. Now it was clear: The devastation was a protest demonstration staged by two militant cats.

The culprits themselves were asleep on the bunk, Yum Yum curled up in a tight ball and Koko stretched full length in a posture of complete exhaustion. When Qwilleran unfolded the linen napkin, however, noses were twitching and ears were alerted, and the two reprobates reported to the kitchen to claim—in a bedlam of baritone and soprano yowls—their escalopes de veau sautées à l'estragon.

"Only a complete sucker would give you a feast after a performance like that," Qwilleran told them.

After straightening the pictures and shoveling up the Fishy Fritters from the four corners of the room, he put on his slippers, lit a pipeful of tobacco, and sat down at his typewriter to list his impressions of the Toledo Tombs and the food foibles of the meritorious gastronome.

Not without apprehension he glanced at the sheet of paper that he regularly left in the machine, and there he saw one word, neatly typed. He adjusted his glasses and leaned closer. It was in lower case this time . . . a single incredible word: *dog*!

In astonishment Qwilleran turned to look at the cat who was industriously licking his paw and washing his face. "Koko!" he said. "This is *too much*!"

SEVEN

QWILLERAN INTENDED TO set the alarm clock Wednesday night, but he forgot, and on Thursday morning he was awakened instead by a rasping noise at the window. Koko and Yum Yum were sitting on the sill, chattering like squirrels at the pigeons outside the glass, while the birds had the effrontery to strut up and down the outer ledge within inches of the two quivering black noses.

Qwilleran awoke with a sense of loss. Did it mean that Joy had gone for good? Or was it merely coincidence that Koko had typed "30," the old newspaper symbol for the end of a story?

Suddenly he recalled the latest message in the typewriter. Coincidence or not, it was fantastic!

"*D-O-G*," he said aloud, and he leaped out of bed with an urgent question on his mind.

He intended to ask Robert Maus at the breakfast table but missed him. He asked Mrs. Marron; she was of no help. He asked Hixie when she reported for ham and eggs and country fries with cinnamon toast, but she had not the faintest idea. Dan Graham failed to appear for breakfast, and when Qwilleran telephoned the pottery later, there was no answer. Finally he called Robert Maus at his office.

"I regret to say that . . . it escapes my memory," the attorney said, "but allow me to consult a copy of the contract."

Qwilleran mumbled an excuse about writing something and needing the information in a hurry.

"No," said Maus after consulting the files. "I see no evidence of a middle name or initial."

Qwilleran phoned Arch Riker at the office and told him about the three-letter word in the typewriter. He said, "I was sure Dan Graham was the type who'd have a middle name like Otho or Oglebert, and I thought Koko might have been trying to tell me something. He's come up with some clues in the past that were no less fantastic."

"I'm glad he's learning to spell," Riker said. "In another six months he should be able to take over your column. How was your dinner last night?"

"Fine, but I didn't learn much. Maus gave me an unlikely story about how he got his black eye."

"Coming downtown for lunch?"

"No, I want to stay home and write my review of the Toledo Tombs. This gourmet racket is full of absurdities, and it's going to be hard to strike the right note—halfway between adulation and a horse laugh."

"Don't offend any restaurant owners," Arch warned him, "or the advertising department will be on my neck . . . Any news about Joy?"

"No. Nothing."

Qwilleran had another reason for wanting to stay home: to be near the phone in case she called. He knew it was too soon to expect a message in the mail; she had been gone hardly more than twenty-four hours. And yet he rushed downstairs when the mail delivery came at eleven o'clock and was disappointed to find nothing in his slot in the foyer. Then he convinced himself that any communication from Joy would be addressed to his office; she would be smart enough for that! A letter in her handwriting would be too easily recognized at Maus Haus. He wondered if the post office was equipped to cope with a letter addressed to "Juu Qwwww" at the "Duuy Fwxwu."

He spent the next hour at his typewriter, trying to write a slyly objective report on the Toledo Tombs. After several fruitless starts, he abandoned that subject and began a profile of Robert Maus—with his pride (sharp knives, lots of butter) and his numerous prejudices. Maus abhorred tea bags, pressure cookers, canned fruit cocktail, bottled mayonnaise, instant coffee, iceberg lettuce, monosodium glutamate, eggs poached in geometric shapes, New England boiled dinners, and anything resembling a smorgasbord, salad bar, or all-you-can-eat buffet.

Once or twice Qwilleran stopped and listened. He thought he could hear someone singing. It was rare to hear live song—not radio and not television. Somewhere a man was singing a Scottish air, and the newsman's Mackintosh blood responded.

Qwilleran was poking at the keys, quoting Maus on the horror of potatoes baked in foil, when there came a knock on the apartment door. Standing in the hall was his elderly neighbor with her white hair and floury face powder, her crossword puzzle and abundance of costume jewelry.

"Forgive me for intruding," Miss Roop said, fingering her three strands of beads, "but this puzzle has me stumped, and I thought you might have a good dictionary, being a writer and all. I need an eleven-letter word for a kind of orchid. The first letter is *c*, and it ends in *m*."

"Cypripedium," said Qwilleran. He spelled it for her.

Miss Roop gasped, and a look of adoration crept into her small blue wrinkle-framed eyes. "Why—why—why, you are remarkable, Mr. Qwilleran!"

He accepted the compliment without revealing the truth. He had learned the word while playing a dictionary game with Koko a few months before. "Will you come in?" he asked.

She started to back away. "Oh, you're probably busy writing one of your wonderful columns." But her eyes seemed eager.

"It's about time I took a breather. Come on in."

"You're sure it's all right?" She glanced down the hall in both directions before stepping quickly into the apartment with a guilty little shrug.

Qwilleran closed the door behind her, and when she looked apprehensive he explained that he must keep the cats from running into the hall. Koko and Yum Yum were sunning themselves on the blue cushion atop the dining table. Miss Roop glanced at them and stiffened perceptibly.

Koko was stretched full length, and Yum Yum was playing with his tail. He tantalized her by slapping it this way and that, and she grabbed it whenever it came within reach. Airborne cat hairs could be seen glistening in the shaft of sunlight that slanted through the studio window.

The relentless daylight also emphasized the two sets of wrinkles on Miss Roop's forehead, caused by the habit of raising her eyebrows.

Koko caught her disapproving stare and stopped playing games. He rolled over, lifted one hind leg and proceeded to lick the base of his tail. The visitor quickly turned away.

"Will you have a chair?" Qwilleran offered her one of the dining chairs, guessing that she liked to sit up straight. He also offered to make a cup of instant coffee, but she declined hastily as if he had made an indecent suggestion.

Mischievously he asked, "Something stronger?"

"Mr. Qwilleran," she said firmly, "I might as well tell you right now that I disapprove of drinking."

"I don't drink either," he admitted in his best

chummy tone, without adding the grim reason why.

Again she beamed at him with so much warmth that she embarrassed herself and began to talk self-consciously—too much, too loud, and too fast. "I love my work. Mr. Hashman was a brilliant man, rest his soul. He taught me everything I know about restaurant management. He sold out a long time ago, and now the Heavenly Hash Houses are a very big fast-food chain; you probably know that. They're owned by three brilliant businessmen—"

"Perhaps I should write a column on the history of the Hash Houses, since they originated in this city." Qwilleran told himself it would be a neat way of sidestepping the quality of the food. "Would you be willing to be interviewed?"

"Oh, dear, no! Don't mention me! I'd rather you would write about the three brilliant men who expanded the chain from three restaurants to eighty-nine."

All uniformly mediocre, thought Qwilleran. He reached for his pipe and then changed his mind, convinced that his visitor would disapprove. With circumspection he attempted to pump her for information. "I'm hoping to write several stories on the gourmets who live at Maus Haus. Do you have any suggestions as to where I should start?"

"Oh, they're all interesting individuals, take my word for it," she said enthusiastically.

"Certainly a varied group. Do they all get along well?"

"Oh, yes, they're lovely people, all very agreeable."

"How about Max Sorrel? Is he a success as a restaurateur?"

"Oh, he's an excellent businessman. I admire Mr. Sorrel greatly."

"Seems to have an eye for the ladies."

"He's a handsome man, with a charming personality, and very fastidious."

Qwilleran felt he was holding a conversation with a computer. He cleared his throat and tried another approach. "You weren't at dinner Tuesday night, but there was a flare-up at the table. William was scolded for incompetence."

"We should all make allowances for youth," Miss Roop said firmly. "He's a nice boy—very friendly. I'm an old lady with white hair, but he talks to me as if we were the same age."

Qwilleran had always had a faculty for inducing people to talk frankly. The look of concern in his eyes and the downward curve of his heavy mustache combined to make him appear sympathetic and sincere, even when he was purely inquisitive, but his technique failed to work with Charlotte Roop. He merely learned that Rosemary was attractive, Hixie amusing, and Robert Maus brilliant—absolutely brilliant.

"I suppose you know," he said, attacking the subject with less delicacy, "that we've lost one of our dinner companions. Mrs. Graham has left her husband—rather suddenly and mysteriously."

Miss Roop raised her chin primly. "I never listen to gossip, Mr. Qwilleran."

"I hope nothing unfortunate has happened to her," he persisted. "I heard a scream the night she disappeared, and it worries me."

"Mrs. Graham is perfectly all right, I'm sure," said Miss Roop. "We must always maintain an optimistic attitude and think constructive thoughts."

"Do you know her well?"

"We've had many friendly conversations, and she has taught me a great deal about her art. I admire her tremendously. A clever woman! And her husband is such a sweet man. They're a lovely couple."

A peculiar noise came from Koko, who had jumped from the table and was looking for an empty shoe. Qwilleran scooped him up and rushed him into the bathroom.

"Excuse me," he said to his guest when the crisis was past. "Koko just chucked his breakfast. He must have a hair ball."

Miss Roop gave Koko a look of faint distaste.

"I wonder what happened to Mrs. Graham's cat," Qwilleran remarked. "She was all broken up about losing him."

"She will rise above it. She is a sensible woman, with remarkably strong character."

"Is that so? I've been told she is capricious and a little scatterbrained."

"I beg to differ! I have seen her at work. She knows what she wants, and she takes endless pains to achieve it. One day she was sitting at the wheel, spinning a pot, as they say—or should I say *casting* a pot?"

"Throwing a pot," Qwilleran corrected her.

"Yes, she was throwing a pot on the wheel, pumping the machine with her dainty little foot, and I asked her why she did not use the electric wheel. It would be so much easier and more efficient. She said, 'I'd rather work harder and produce an object that has my own personality in the clay.' That was a beautiful thought. She is a real artist." Miss Roop rose to leave. "I have stayed too long. I'm keeping you from your work." And when Qwilleran remonstrated, she added, "No, I must go downstairs and get a bite to eat."

When Charlotte Roop was gone, Qwilleran said to Koko, "Did you hear what she said about the wheel?"

"Yow!" said Koko, who was back on the table, washing himself in the sunlight.

"Dan said he saved Joy from a serious injury by throwing *the switch*. A slight discrepancy, don't you think?"

Koko nodded in agreement, it seemed, or was he merely licking the pale patch of fur on his breast?

"I'd like to figure out a way to sneak you into that pottery," Qwilleran said. "I'll bet you could sniff out some clues."

More than once in the past Koko had led the way into a highly revealing situation, but if the cat had a sixth sense about suspicious behavior, Qwilleran's sensitive mustache had an equal awareness. Many a time it had alerted him to bad news, hidden danger, and even unsuspected crime.

Now he was experiencing the same disturbing quiver on his upper lip. It was telling him that something dire had happened to Joy. It was telling him that Joy was not alive. He didn't want to believe his hunch. He *refused* to believe his hunch.

EIGHT

FOR QWILLERAN THE day seemed interminable. He skipped lunch. At noon Rosemary stopped at his door with a ball of yarn; she had been tidying her knitting basket and thought the cats would enjoy some exercise with a ball of yarn. Qwilleran invited her to come in, but she was on her way to work. In the afternoon the sun disappeared behind a bank of gray clouds, and the cold light flooding through the huge studio window drenched the apartment in gloom. The cats felt the chill. Ignoring the yarn, they crept behind the books in the bookcase and found a cozier place for their afternoon nap.

Qwilleran was thankful when the time came to leave for the Stilton Hotel. He needed a change of scene and a change of thought, and he was glad, somewhat, that he had invited the babbling Hixie Rice. On the way to the hotel he stopped at the office to open his mail, and a fleeting impulse sent him to the *Fluxion* library to pick up an old clip file on the River Road pottery . . . the Penniman Pottery, as it was originally known.

He met Hixie in the hotel lobby. It seemed to the newsman that she was exhibiting desperate gaiety with her cherry red suit and shrimp pink hat laden with straw carrots, turnips, and radishes.

"That's a tasty *chapeau*," Qwilleran remarked.

"*Merci, monsieur*." She fluttered her double set of eyelashes. "I'm glad you like it."

"I didn't say that."

"Oh, you're a kidder!" Hixie gave him a playful shove. "I couldn't resist the straw *légumes*. You know me! . . . Do you speak French?"

"Only enough to keep out of trouble in Paris."

"I'm taking a Berlitz course. Say something in French."

"Camembert, Roquefort, Brie," said Qwilleran.

The annual Choose Cheese celebration was being hosted by the cheese industry in the hotel ballroom. The hundred or more guests, however, were patronizing the free bar and ignoring the long table of assorted cheeses.

"This is a typical press party," Qwilleran explained. "About six of the guests are members of the working press, and nobody knows who the others are or why they were invited."

He smoked his pipe and sampled a Danish cheese made with skim milk. Hixie sipped a Manhattan and sampled the Brie, Camembert, Cheshire, Edam, Gorgonzola, Gouda, Gruyère, Herkimer, Liederkranz, Mozzarella, Muenster, Parmesan, Port du Salut, and Roquefort.

"Is that all you're going to eat, for gosh sake?" she asked.

"I might take a little Roquefort home to Koko," Qwilleran said and then added, "We had an unexpected visitor today—Miss Roop. I sense that she disapproves of cats. Koko didn't approve of her, either."

"Charlotte disapproves of *everything*," said Hixie. "Smoking, drinking, gambling, divorce, short skirts, shaggy dog stories, foreigners, motorcycles, movies with unhappy endings, politicians, gum-chewing, novels written after 1910, overtipping of waiters, and sex."

That kind always has a skeleton in the closet, Qwilleran thought. "Has there ever been any romance in her life?" he asked his well-informed companion.

"Who knows? I suspect she was secretly in love with Hash House Hashman. He's been dead for fifteen years, but she still talks about him all the time."

Qwilleran chewed his pipe stem thoughtfully. "Did you ever wonder what happened to Joy Graham's cat?"

Hixie shrugged. "Ran away, I suppose. Got picked up. Got run over by a bus. Fell in the river. Choose one of the above."

"Do you like pets?"

"If they don't cause trouble or tie you down too much. I bought myself a canary, but he seems to be a deaf-mute. That's just my luck. I'm a born loser."

Qwilleran sliced a wedge of Norwegian Gjetost and presented it to her on a cracker. "I suppose you know that Joy has disappeared."

"Yes, I heard she left him." For a moment Hixie's jovial expression changed to one Qwilleran could not identify, but her face quickly brightened again. "Try this Westphalian Sauermilch, *mon ami. C'est formidable!*"

Qwilleran obliged and remarked that it was a little immature. It had not quite achieved total putrefaction. He was determined, however, not to let her change the subject. "Did you ever see Joy throw a pot on the wheel?" he asked.

"No, but she almost threw a pot at my head once. I accidentally broke a dumb-looking pitcher she'd made, and after that I wasn't exactly welcome in the pottery."

"We've got a colorful tribe at Maus Haus. What kind of guy is Max Sorrel?"

"A confirmed bachelor," Hixie groaned. "His only love affair is with that big fat restaurant . . . Poor Max! He's got the legendary heart of gold, and he doesn't deserve the trouble he's having."

"What kind of trouble?"

"Don't you know? He may lose his restaurant. He's even had to sell his boat! He has—or he *did* have—a gorgeous thirty-six-foot cruiser that he used to tie up behind Maus Haus."

"What's the problem?"

"You mean you haven't heard the rumors?"

Qwilleran scowled and shook his head, professionally humiliated because rumors were circulating and he, a member of the Press Club, was in the dark.

"People are saying all kinds of absurd things. Like, Max's head chef has a horrible disease. Like, a customer found something unspeakable in his soup. Sick jokes."

"Sounds like a poison tongue campaign."

"It's rotten, because Max runs a meticulously clean restaurant. And yet the rumors have mushroomed, and the customers are staying away in droves."

"I thought the Golden Lamb Chop had a sophisticated clientele. They should know that the Board of Health—"

"Nobody *believes* the rumors, but café society and the gambling crowd won't patronize a spot that's being laughed at. And they've been Max's best customers."

"Does he have any idea how the thing started?"

She shook her head. "He's very well liked all over town. I told him he ought to get one of the papers to print a story about it, so he could deny everything publicly, but he said that would only attract more unwelcome attention. He's hoping it will blow over before he goes completely broke."

"It's slander," Qwilleran said. "He's got a case if he can find out who's behind it."

"That's what Robert says, but Max can't trace a thing."

Qwilleran had considered inviting Hixie to dinner—even after all the cheese—but he changed his mind. He wanted to go to the Golden Lamb Chop, and he wanted to go alone. Taking her home in a taxi, he sensed her disappointment.

"Do you like baseball?" he asked. "I can get seats in the press box some weekend, if you'd like to go." He was being noble. If his friends in the press box saw him with this overweight, overdressed, overexpressive date, they'd never let him live it down.

"Sure, I like baseball. Especially the hot dogs."

"Any particular team you'd like to see?"

"Whoever's at the bottom of the league. I like to root for the underdog."

When Qwilleran returned to Number Six to give the cats some turkey with a garnish of Roquefort, he was greeted by a scene of incredible beauty. The apartment had been transformed into a work of art. The cats had found Rosemary's ball of gray yarn and had spun a web that enmeshed every article of furniture in the room. They had rolled the ball across the floor, tossed it over chairs, looped it around table legs, carried it up to the desk and around the typewriter and down again to the floor, hooking it in the jaws of the bear before repeating the same basic design with variations. Now the cats sat on the bookcase, as motionless as statuary, contemplating their creation.

Qwilleran had seen string sculpture at the museum that was less artful, and it was a shame to destroy it, but the crisscrossing strands made it impossible to move about the room. He found the end of the yarn and rewound it—an athletic performance that took half an hour and burned off an ounce of his avoirdupois. This time he put the ball of yarn away in the desk drawer. Then he went to dinner—alone.

The Golden Lamb Chop occupied a prominent corner where State Street, River Road, and the expressway converged. The building was a nineteenth-century landmark, having been the depot for interurban trolleys before the automobile came on the scene. Now the interior had a golden glow, like money: gold damask on the walls, gold silk shades on the table lamps, ornate gilt frames on the oil paintings. The floor was thickly carpeted in a gold plush, spongy enough to turn an unwary ankle and uniquely patterned with a lamb chop motif in metallic gold threads.

At the door to the main dining room Qwilleran was

greeted by Max Sorrel—hand on heart. His well-shaped head was freshly shaved; his dark suit and candy-striped shirt were crisp as cornflakes.

"You alone?" the restaurateur asked, flashing a professional smile with the minty fragrance of toothpaste and mouthwash. "Just hang your coat in the checkroom. We don't have a hatcheck girl tonight." He seated the newsman at a table near the entrance. "I want you to be the guest of the house. Understand?"

"No, this is on the *Daily Fluxion*. Let them pay for it."

"We'll argue about that later. Mind if I join you—in between seating customers? We're not very busy on weeknights, and I've given my maître d' a little vacation."

The proprietor took a seat where he could keep a hopeful eye on the entrance. Thirty empty tables stood waiting in their gold tablecloths, with gold napkins folded precisely and tucked into the amber goblets.

"How many can you seat?" Qwilleran asked.

"Two hundred, counting the private dining room upstairs. What'll you have to drink?"

"Just tomato juice."

Sorrel called a waiter. There was only one of them in evidence. "One tomato juice and one rye and soda, Charlie, and get me a clean glass, will you?" He handed over a goblet on which a drop of detergent had left a spot. "If there's anything I can't stand," he told Qwilleran, "it's spots on the glassware. What'll you have to eat? I recommend the rack of lamb."

"Sounds good," Qwilleran said, "but I may have to take some of it home in a doggie bag. I'm on a diet."

"What for a first course? Vichyssoise? Herring in sour cream?"

"Better make it a half-grapefruit."

Qwilleran started to light his pipe, and Sorrel pushed an amber glass ashtray toward him, after examining it for blemishes. "Know how we clean ashtrays here?" he said. "With wet teabags. It's the best way . . . Excuse me a moment."

A couple had entered the empty dining room, looking bewildered, as if they had come on the wrong night.

"You don't have a reservation?" Sorrel asked them with a frown. He hesitated. He consulted a ledger. He did some crossing out and some writing in. Finally—with a convincing show of magnanimity and a buttery smile for the lady—he consented to give them a table, seating them in a large front window in full view of passing traffic. He explained to them that the regular crowd was late because of the ball game, as he removed from their table a gold tent-card that said "Reserved."

When the grapefruit was served, Sorrel watched Qwilleran spoon it out of the rind. "You unhappy about something?" he asked the newsman.

Qwilleran gave him a questioning frown.

"I can tell by the way you eat your grapefruit. You're going around it counterclockwise. Did you ever watch people eat grapefruit? The happy ones eat clockwise."

"Curious theory."

"Do you secretly wiggle your toes inside your shoes when you eat something good?"

"I don't know, and I'm not sure I want to know."

"I can tell a lot about people by watching them eat—how they break their rolls, spoon their soup, cut their meat—even the way they chew."

"How do you size up the motley crew at Maus Haus?" Qwilleran asked.

"Interesting bunch. Hixie—she's got a lot of ginger, but she's getting panicky. She wants to get married in the worst way. Rosemary—she looks like a perfect lady, but don't be too sure. William—there's something weasely about that boy. He's not on the up-and-up. I can tell by the way he holds his fork. How do you size him up?"

"He's okay. Strikes me as an amusing kid, with a lot of healthy curiosity."

"Maybe I shouldn't tell you this," Sorrel confided, "because I don't want to stir up trouble, but I saw him letting himself into your apartment last night around eight o'clock, and he was looking kind of sneaky. Did you authorize him to go into your apartment?"

"How did you happen to see him?" Qwilleran wanted to know. "I thought you worked every night."

"Well, we had an accident in the kitchen, and some cocktail sauce got splashed on my shirt. I rushed home to change. . . . Excuse me."

The restaurateur jumped up to seat a party of four, obviously tourists, while Qwilleran said to himself, Wouldn't a fastidious guy like Sorrel keep an extra shirt on hand at his place of business?

When the lamb was served, looking like the Rock of Gibraltar, Qwilleran remarked, "Do you know Joy Graham has left her husband?"

"No! When did that happen?"

"Early yesterday morning."

"Is she getting a divorce?"

"I don't know. She left no explanation, according to Dan. Just disappeared."

"I'm not surprised," Sorrel said. "I wouldn't blame her for unloading that ape. She's got a lot on the ball." His eyes glowed with appreciation. "I'm not strongly in favor of marriage myself. There are better ways to live. People marry, divorce, marry, divorce. It's not respectable."

"Did you ever watch her work with clay?"

"Me? No, sir! I've never set foot in that pottery. I took one look at all the dust and mud, and I knew that wasn't for me." His expression changed from one of distaste to one of approval. "So the little cabbage got the hell out, did she? Good for her!"

"It mystifies me why she'd depart in the middle of the night—in a violent rainstorm," Qwilleran said.

"Sure you don't want a baked potato with sour cream and chives?" his host urged.

"Thanks, no . . . And another mystery," Qwilleran went on, "is what happened to her cat. He was a neutered longhair, and they don't go roaming the countryside in search of adventure; they sit around like sofa pillows. Do you have any ideas about what happened to that cat?"

Sorrel turned the color of borscht, and the veins in his temples seemed ready to burst.

"What's the matter?" Qwilleran asked in alarm. "Are you all right?"

The restaurateur mopped his brow with a gold napkin and lowered his voice. "I thought for a minute you were riding me—about that ugly story that's going around town." He gave the newsman a wary glance. "You haven't heard?"

Qwilleran shook his head.

"I'm being persecuted. A lot of dirty rumors are drifting around, and I don't mind telling you they're hurting my business. This place should be three-quarters full on Thursday night. Look at it! Six customers!"

"What kind of rumors?"

Sorrel winced. "That I use cat meat in the twelve-ounce chopped sirloin—and all that kind of rot. I could tell you worse, only it would spoil your dinner. Why don't they say I've got a gambling den in the back room? Why don't they say I keep girls upstairs? *That* I could take! But they're getting me where it hurts. Me! The guy who's known for keeping the cleanest kitchen in the city!"

"Any idea who could be circulating these rumors?" Qwilleran asked. "What would their motive be?"

Sorrel shrugged. "I don't know. Nobody seems to know. But it looks like a plot—especially after what happened Tuesday night."

"What happened?"

"My kitchen caught fire in the middle of the night. The police called me, and I came back downtown. It had to be arson. I don't leave grease around. I don't use any inflammable cleaners . . . Let me tell you: If anything happened to this place I'd crack up! I love this restaurant! The drapes cost forty dollars a yard. The carpet was custom-woven. Where did you ever see a carpet with a lamb chop design?"

Qwilleran had to admit the floor-covering was unusual. "Does anyone have a grudge against you—personally?"

"Me? I've got a million friends. Ask anybody. I couldn't think of an enemy if you paid me."

"How about your employees? Have you fired anyone who might be out for revenge?"

"No, I've always treated my people right, and they like me. Ask any one of them. Ask Charlie." The waiter was bringing the coffee. "Charlie, do I treat you right? Tell this man—he's from the newspaper. Do I treat everyone right?"

"Yes, *sir*," said Charlie in a flat voice.

Qwilleran declined Sorrel's offer of a dessert from the cart, which offered rum cream pie, banana Bavarian, pecan caramel custard, strawberry shortcake, and chocolate mousse, and he left the restaurant with the rest of his lamb wrapped in aluminum foil. He crossed River Road to hail a westbound taxi, but a bus came along and he climbed aboard.

It was one of the slow evening buses, and the leisurely speed and the drone of the engine were conducive to meditation . . . Why were women attracted to men with shiny bald heads? Max Sorrel was obviously attractive to the opposite sex. Had he incurred the enmity of a jealous rival? A jealous husband? . . . Had there been something between Joy and Max? If Dan resented it, would he have the wit to conduct a successful smear campaign against the Golden Lamb Chop? . . . Max had seemed surprised to learn of Joy's disappearance, but he was a good actor. He might have been lying . . . And how about the departure of Max's convertible at three in the morning? The restaurant fire would account for that—if the story of the fire happened to be true. Qwilleran made a mental note to verify it . . . As for William's surreptitious visit to Number Six, Qwilleran was not unduly concerned. The key rack in the kitchen was readily accessible, and the houseboy had probably wanted to see the cats. William had a healthy curiosity —a virtue, from a newsman's point of view. He also had brash nerve and a glib tongue and an easygoing personality. Qwilleran and Riker had been the same way when they were in their twenties, before their exuberance was curbed by disappointments and compromises and the old newsman's realization that there is never anything really new.

Wrapped in his thoughts, Qwilleran rode a mile beyond Maus Haus and had to wait for another slow bus traveling in the opposite direction.

When he finally arrived home, he found some changes in the Great Hall. The long dining table and the high-backed chairs had been moved aside, and the area was dotted with pedestals of various heights. In the center of the room a few railroad ties had been arranged on the floor to form a large square, and Dan Graham was down on hands and knees filling the square with pebbles. Alone in the vast hall, pushing the pebbles this way and that as if their placement mattered profoundly, he made a sad picture of insignificance, Qwilleran thought.

"How's it going, Mr. Granam?" he asked.

"Slow," said the potter. "It's not much fun, doing the setup alone." He stood up and massaged his back, while viewing the pebbles critically. "My best pieces will be displayed on pedestals in this square. I'm gonna surprise this city, you can betcha boots."

"How soon are we going to see the new pots?"

"Maybe Monday or Tuesday. I've got some sweet patooties cooling in the kiln right now. Did you talk to anybody at the paper?"

"Everything is under control. Don't worry about it," Qwilleran said, although he had forgotten to tell Riker about anything but Joy's disappearance. "Any news from your wife?"

"Nope. Not a word. But it wouldn't surprise me if she came back in time for the hoopla on Wednesday. We sent out three hundred invitations last week. Should be a swell party. I'm shooting the works—bubble water, horses' duvvers, the right stuff, if you know what I mean. The critics better come, that's all I've got to say . . . Here, let me show you something." Graham reached around to his hip pocket and once more brought forth the yellowed clipping about his past glories.

When Qwilleran went upstairs to Number Six, he

found the cats waiting for him, with anticipation in the cock of their ears.

"Koko, where is that guy getting the money to buy champagne for three hundred guests," Qwilleran asked him.

The cat's eyes were like large black cherries in the lamplight—expressionless, yet holding all the answers to all the questions ever asked.

Qwilleran arranged his coat over the back of a chair and whipped off his tie. Yum Yum watched the tie with bright, hopeful eyes. He usually switched it through the air for her to jump at and catch, but tonight he was too preoccupied to play. Instead he sat in the big chair, put on his glasses, and opened the packet of clippings from the *Fluxion* library.

Robert Maus had not exaggerated. Every five years the *Fluxion* had resurrected the story of the mysterious deaths at the pottery, most likely to embarrass the *Morning Rampage*. The rival newspaper was still financed by the Penniman family. It had been old Hugh Penniman who built the strange art center and hobnobbed with its arty residents

The stories, written in the old-fashioned Sunday supplement style, related how "a handsome young sculptor" by the name of Mortimer Mellon had fallen in love with "the lovely Helen Maude Hake," a lady potter. She, alas, happened to be the "protégée" of Hugh Penniman, "the well-known philanthropist." Following a "wild party" at the pottery, the body of the "lovelorn sculptor" was found in the river, and a verdict of accidental death was pronounced by the coroner. Not satisfied with the disposition of the case, reporters from the *Fluxion* attempted to interview other artists at the pottery, but the "slovenly Bohemians" showed "an insolent lack of cooperation." Soon afterward the episode came to "its final tragic end" when "the lovely Helen" took her own life, following Mortimer "to a watery grave." She left a suicide note that was never made public.

Just as Qwilleran finished reading, he heard a thud at

the opposite end of the room, and he turned to see a book with a red cover lying open and face down on the floor. With a softer thump Koko landed on the floor beside it and started nosing it across the slippery tile floor.

"Bad cat!" Qwilleran scolded. It was a library book —an old one, none too solid in the spine. "The librarian will have you shot! Bad cat!" Qwilleran repeated.

As he scowled his displeasure, he saw Koko slowly arch his back and flatten his ears. The cat's brown tail stiffened, and he began to step around the book in a strange long-legged dance. He circled the book once, twice, three times, and Qwilleran felt a chill in the pit of his stomach. Once before, in an icy courtyard, he had seen Koko perform that ritual. Once before, the cat had walked around and around and around, and the thing he circled was a body.

Now it was a book he was circling—an old red book titled *The Ancient Art of Potting*. The silence was broken only by the mournful sound of a boat whistle on the river.

NINE

BEFORE GOING TO bed Thursday night Qwilleran telephoned the *Fluxion*'s night man at police headquarters and asked him to check for unidentified bodies dragged from the river in the last forty-eight hours.

Kendall called back with the information. "There was one," he said. "Male. Caucasian. About sixty years old. Is that your boy?"

Qwilleran slept fitfully that night, and between his restless moments he dreamed about seaweed—great curtains of seaweed undulating with the motion of the waves. Then it became a head of green hair swirling in dirty brown water.

When he awoke in the morning he had a feeling that his bones had turned to jelly. He dressed wearily, ignoring the cats, and they seemed to sense that he was preoccupied; they kept out of his way. It was when he started downstairs for a steadying cup of coffee that he walked into the situation that stiffened his spirit. He met Robert Maus on the stairs.

The attorney stopped and faced him squarely, and the newsman saw that the black eye had faded to a banana-peel yellow. Maus gave the impression that he was about to say something momentous, and after a few long seconds it came out: "Mr. Qwilleran, do you, by any chance, have a moment of your valuable time to spare?"

"I guess so."

They went to Maus's apartment, a comfortable place done in English antiques and broccoli-green leather, with much polished brass and steel.

The attorney bowed and motioned Qwilleran to a Bank of England chair. "The matter I have to discuss," he said, "concerns Mrs. Graham. I find it somewhat, shall I say, painful to approach you in this manner, and you must not, under any circumstance, consider this an accusation or even a reproach. However . . . a matter has been brought to my attention, signifying that a word with you at this time would not be amiss—in consideration of the apprehensions I entertain concerning what I humbly describe as . . . the respectability of this establishment."

"What the devil is the problem?" Qwilleran demanded.

The attorney raised a protesting hand. "Nothing that could be termed—in any real and active sense—a problem, I assure you, but rather a situation that has been brought to my cognizance . . . and in apprising you of the fact I am seeking neither confirmation nor denial . . . my only interest being to maintain good relationships . . ."

"Okay, what's this all about?" Qwilleran snapped. "Let's have it!"

Maus paused as if counting to ten and then stated slowly and carefully, "Mr. Graham, whom you have met . . . is under the impression . . . that his wife received considerable financial aid from you . . . to make her departure possible. I am not, I repeat—"

Qwilleran jumped to his feet and walked impatiently

across the Oriental rug. "How did I know she was going to run off? She was going to get a divorce. You know that as well as I do. And one of your legal buddies had his hand out for more than she could afford. And if Dan has a complaint, why doesn't he come and see me about it?"

Maus lowered the pitch of his voice and spoke apologetically. "He fears—whether with or without cause, I do not know—that a confrontation might, shall we say, impair his chances of favorable comment in the . . . publication you represent."

"Or—to put it more honestly—he's hoping his accusation will make me feel so guilty that I'll knock myself out to get a picture of his pots on the front page. It's not the first time I've run up against that simple-minded strategy. It's a stupid move, and I may get mad enough to forget the free publicity entirely. You can tell him that!"

Maus raised both hands. "Let us preserve our equanimity, at all costs, and bear in mind that my only motive in intervening is to prevent any taint of . . . scandal."

"You're apt to have something worse than scandal on your hands!" Qwilleran roared as he stormed out of the apartment.

He was still irritable when he arrived at the *Fluxion* to pick up his paycheck and open his mail. He went through his mail hopefully each day, and his pulse still skipped a beat every time the telephone jangled, although instinct told him there would be no word from Joy.

In the feature department he said to Riker, "Come on down to the coffee shop. I've got a few things to tell you."

"Before I forget it," the feature editor said, "would you attend a press luncheon this noon and write a few inches for tomorrow's paper? They're introducing a new product."

"What kind of product?"

"A new dog food."

"Dog food! Isn't that stretching my responsibilities as gourmet reporter?"

"Well, you haven't done anything else to earn your paycheck this week—not that I can see . . . Come on. What's on your mind?"

The *Fluxion* coffee shop was in the basement, and at midmorning it was the noisiest and therefore the most private conference room in the building. Newspaper deadlines being what they were, the compositors were having their dinner, the pressmen were having their lunch, the advertising representatives were having breakfast, and the clerical workers were having their first coffee break. The concrete-walled room shook with the roar of nearby presses; customers were shouting at one another; counter girls yelled orders; cooks barked replies; busboys slammed dishes; and a radio was bleating without an audience for the reason that it could not possibly be heard. The resulting din made the coffee shop highly desirable for confidential conversations; only mouth-to-ear shouts were audible.

The two men ordered coffee, and the feature editor asked for a chocolate-frosted doughnut as well. "What's up?" he shouted in Qwilleran's ear.

"About Dan Graham! That story he told!" Qwilleran shouted back. "I think it's a lie!"

"What story?"

"About Joy's hair getting caught in the wheel."

"Why would he lie?"

Qwilleran shook his head ominously. "I think something's happened to Joy. I don't think she ran away."

"But you saw a car—"

"Max Sorrel's! Fire at his restaurant!"

The waitress banged two coffees on the counter.

"This hunch of yours—" Riker yelled.

"Wretched thought!"

"Wretched *what*?"

"Wretched *thought*!"

"You don't mean . . ." The editor's face was pained.

"I don't know." Qwilleran touched his mustache nervously. "It's a possibility."

"But where's the body?"

"Maybe in the river!"

The two men stared into the depths of their coffee cups and let the deafening cacophony of the coffee shop assault their numb eardrums.

"Another thing!" Qwilleran shouted after a while. "Dan knows about my check! The seven-fifty!"

"How'd he find out?"

Qwilleran shrugged.

"What are you going to do?"

"Keep asking questions!"

Riker nodded gravely.

"Don't tell Rosie!"

"What?"

"*Don't tell Rosie*! Not yet!"

"Right!" —

"Upset her!"

"Right!"

Qwilleran survived the dog food luncheon and wrote a mildly witty piece about it for the feature page, comparing the simplicity of canine cuisine with the gustatory demands of catdom. Then he went home to feed Koko and Yum Yum, but first he stopped at a delicatessen. He hungrily eyed the onion rolls, chopped chicken livers, and pickled herring, but he steeled himself and bought only a chub for the cats. He had abandoned once and for all his experiment with canned cat food.

He had slipped a note under William's door that morning, inviting the houseboy to have dinner with him at a new restaurant called the Petrified Bagel, and now the young man met him in the Great Hall and accepted with glee.

"Let's leave about six-thirty," Qwilleran suggested. "Is that too early?"

"No, that's good," said William. "I have to go over to my mother's house after. You don't have a car, do you? We can take mine."

Qwilleran went upstairs, taking three of the stone steps at a time. Suddenly he was filled with an unwarranted exhilaration. The bewilderment was over; he had a job to do. Now that he felt certain his hunch was correct—now that he could proceed with his unofficial investigation—his spirit rose to the challenge. Instead of grief for Joy he felt a fierce loyalty to her memory. And it was the *memory* that he loved, he had to confess. It was Joy Wheatley, age nineteen, who had made his heart beat fast on Monday night—not Joy Graham. Two decades of separation made a difference, he now admitted, even though he had convinced himself for a few days that nothing had changed.

The cats caught his high-key mood and raced about the apartment —up on the bookcase, down to the floor, around the big chair, under the table, up on the captain's bunk—with Yum Yum in the lead and Koko following so close behind that they made a single blur of blond fur. Rounding a curve, she slowed for a fraction of a second, and Koko ran over her. Then she was chasing him.

Qwilleran dodged the hurtling bodies, removed his shoes, and stepped on the scale. He stepped off with a smile of satisfaction. It was a fine spring night. The ventilating panes in the big studio window were open, and the breeze was gentle. Somewhere in or around the building a man's voice could be heard, singing "Loch Lomond," and it gave Qwilleran a moment of nostalgia; it had been his father's favorite.

He met William in the Great Hall; the houseboy had dressed for the occasion in a wrinkled sports coat the color of gravy. A long black limousine of ancient vintage stood quietly rumbling at the front door.

"Looks like a hearse," Qwilleran remarked.

"Best I could get for fifty dollars," William apologized. "I've been warming her up, because she takes a little coaxing before she starts to roll. Open the door easy, or it'll come off."

"Must cost you a fortune in gas."

"I don't use her that much, but she comes in handy for dates. Would you like to drive? Then I can hold the passenger door on."

With Qwilleran behind the wheel, Black Beauty moved majestically down the drive with the authoritative rumbling of a car with a defective muffler. Several times when he glanced in the rearview mirror, he thought he was being followed, but it was only the tail of the limousine looming up in the distance.

The restaurant was in that part of the city known as Junktown, a declining neighborhood that a few enterprising preservationists were trying to restore. A former antique shop on Zwinger Street was now making a brave comeback as a restaurant, and the Petrified Bagel was furnished, appropriately, with junk. Old kitchen chairs and tables, no two alike, were painted in mismatched colors, and the burlap-covered walls were decorated with relics from the city dump, while the waiters appeared to be derelicts recruited from Junktown's bars and alleys.

"The food may not be the greatest," Qwilleran told William, "but it should make a colorful story for my column."

"Who cares, when it's free?" was the houseboy's attitude.

They took a table against the wall, beneath an arrangement of rusty plumbing fixtures, and hardly had they pulled up their chairs when their waiter was upon them.

"What wudjus like?" he asked. "Wudjus like a drink from the bar?" He wore a black suit, a few sizes too large, and a crooked bow tie, and if he had shaved, he had done so with a butter knife.

William said he'd like a beer, and Qwilleran ordered a lemon and seltzer.

"Wudjus say that again?"

"A beer for the gentleman," Qwilleran said, "and I'll have some soda water with a squeeze of lemon." To William he said, "I know this neighborhood. I used to live in the old Spencer mansion on this block—a historic house with a ghost."

"Honest? Did you ever see the ghost?"

"No, but some strange things happened, and it was hard to sort out the pranks of the disembodied lady from the pranks of my cats."

The waiter returned empty-handed. "Wudjus like sugar in that?"

"No, just lemon and soda water."

William said, "How are the cats doing with their typing lessons?"

"You'd never believe it, but Koko actually typed a word the other day. A rather elementary word, but . . ." Qwilleran looked up and caught the Irish twinkle in the houseboy's eye. "You *dog*!" Qwilleran said. "Is that what you were doing in my apartment Wednesday night? My spies saw you sneaking in."

William guffawed loudly. "I wondered how long it would be before you got the picture. I found some caviar in Mickey Maus's refrigerator and took it up to your cats. They liked it."

"Who wouldn't?"

The waiter brought the drinks. "Wudjus like something to go with it?"

Qwilleran shook his head. To William he said, "How did you hit it off with Koko and Yum Yum?"

"The little one ran away, but the big one came out, and we had a lengthy conversation. He talks even more than I do. I like cats. You can't boss them around."

"And you can't win, either. You may think you've put one over on them, but they always come out ahead."

"Wudjus like to see the menu?" The waiter was offering a grease-spotted folder covered in burlap.

"Later," said Qwilleran . . . "How's everything going at art school?"

William shrugged. "I'm going to quit. It's not my bag. My girl's an artist, and she wanted me to go there, but . . . I don't know. After I got out of the service I tried college, but it wasn't for me. You had to *study*! I'd sort of like to be a bartender. Or a waiter at a good place where you get king-size tips."

"Didjus want something?" asked the waiter, who was never out of earshot.

Qwilleran waved him away, but before the man left he rearranged the sticky salt and pepper shakers and whisked an imaginary crumb off the plastic tablecloth.

"What I'd really like," William went on, "I'd like to be a private operator. I read a lot of detective stories, and I think I'd be pretty good at it."

"Investigative work fascinates me, too," Qwilleran confided. "I used to cover the crime beat in Chicago and New York."

"You did? Did you cover any big cases? Did you cover the Valentine's Day massacre?"

"I'm not *that* old, sonny."

"Didn't you ever want to be a detective yourself?"

"Not really." Qwilleran preened his mustache. "But a reporter sharpens his faculty for observation and gets in the habit of asking questions. I've been asking myself questions ever since I came to Maus Haus."

"Like what?"

"Who screamed at three-thirty Wednesday morning? Why was the pottery door locked? How did Maus get his black eye? What happened to Joy Graham's cat? What's happened to Joy Graham?"

"You think something's happened to her?"

The waiter was hovering around the table. "Wudjus like to order now?"

Qwilleran took a deep breath of exasperation. "Yes, bring me some escargots, vichyssoise, boeuf Bourguignon, and a small salade Niçoise."

There was a long silence, then, "Wudjus say that again?"

"Never mind," said Qwilleran. "Just bring me a frozen hamburger, gently warmed, and some canned peas."

William ordered cream of mushroom soup, pot roast with mashed potatoes, and salad with Thousand Island dressing. "Say, is it true you used to be engaged to her?" he asked Qwilleran.

"Joy? That was a long time ago. Who told you?"

William looked wise. "I found out, that's all. Do you still like her?"

"Of course. But not in the same way."

"A lot of people at Maus Haus like her. Ham Hamilton was nuts about her. I think that's why he had himself transferred—to stay out of trouble."

Qwilleran groomed his mustache; another possible clue was gnawing at his upper lip. "Did you hear anything or notice anything unusual the night she disappeared?"

"No, I played gin with Rosemary until ten o'clock. Then she had to take her beauty treatment on her slant board, so I tried to find Hixie, but she was out. I watched TV for a while. Once I heard Dan's car pull out of the carport, but I was in bed by midnight. I have an early class on Wednesdays."

The waiter brought the soup. "Wudjus like some crackers?"

"By the way," Qwilleran asked the houseboy, "do you know what they mean by a 'slob potter'? I've heard Dan called a slob potter."

William's explosive laugh rang through the restaurant. "You mean *slab* potter, although you're not so very far off base. Dan rolls out the clay in flat slabs and builds square and rectangular pieces that way."

"Do you think he's good?"

"Who am I to say? I'm *really* a slob potter . . . This is crummy soup."

"Is it canned?"

"No, worse! It tastes like I made it."

"Dan says he's aiming for big things in New York and Europe."

"Yeah, I know. And I guess he means it. He got a passport in the mail last week."

"He did? How do you know?"

"I was there when the mail came. I *guess* it was a

passport. It was in a thick brown envelope that said 'Passport Office' or something like that in the corner."

The waiter served the main course. "Wudjus like ketchup?"

"No ketchup," said Qwilleran. "No mustard. No steak sauce. No chili sauce."

William said, "If you want to see Mickey Maus have a cat fit, just mention ketchup."

"I hear Maus is a widower. What happened to his wife?"

"She choked to death a couple of years ago. They say she choked on a bone in the chicken Marengo. She was a lot older than Mickey Maus. I think he likes older women. Look at Charlotte!"

"What about Charlotte?"

"I mean, the way he butters her up all the time. At first I thought Charlotte was his mother. Max thinks she's his mistress. Hixie says Mickey Maus is the illegitimate son of Charlotte and that old guy who started the Heavenly Hash business." William howled with merriment.

"I hear Max is having a rough time at the Golden Lamb Chop."

"Too bad. I've got my theories about that, too."

"Like what?"

"Like he goes for chicks, you know, on a wholesale scale. And he doesn't bother to play by the rules."

"You think there might be a jealous husband in the picture?"

"It's just a guess. Hey, why don't you and I open a detective agency? It wouldn't take much capital . . . Look out! Here comes Professor Moriarty again."

"Wudjus like some more butter?" asked the waiter.

For a while Qwilleran concentrated on his hamburger, which had been grilled to the consistency of a steel-belted radial tire, and William concentrated on satisfying his youthful appetite.

"I have to get up at six tomorrow morning," he remarked. "Gotta go to the farmers' market with Mickey."

"I wouldn't mind going along," Qwilleran said. "It might be a story."

"Never been there? It's a gas! Just meet us in the kitchen at six-thirty. Want me to call you?"

"Thanks, but I've got an alarm clock. Three of them, counting the cats."

William ordered strawberry cheesecake for dessert. "Best wallpaper paste I've ever eaten," he said.

Qwilleran ordered black coffee, which was served in a mug with the flavor of detergent lingering on the rim. "By the way," he said, "did you ever watch Joy Graham when she was using the wheel?"

His guest nodded, his mouth full of cheesecake.

"Which wheel did she use?"

"The kick-wheel. Why?"

"Never the electric?"

"No, she has to do everything the hard way, when it comes to pottery. Don't ask me why. I know she's a friend of yours, but she does some wacky things."

"She always did."

"Know what I overheard at the dinner last Monday? She was talking to Tweedledee and Tweedledum—"

"The Penniman brothers?"

William nodded. "She was trying to sell them some old papers she found in the pottery somewhere. She said they could have them for *five thousand dollars*!"

"She was kidding," Qwilleran said, without conviction.

They left the Petrified Bagel after the waiter's final solicitation: "Wudjus like a toothpick?"

Qwilleran went home on the bus. William was going to visit his mother.

"It's her birthday," the houseboy explained, "and I've bought her some cheap perfume. It doesn't matter what you give her; she makes insulting remarks about everything, so what's the use?"

In the Great Hall at Maus Haus, Dan was again working on the exhibit, pushing and pulling massive tables and benches into position for the display of pots. He was humming "Loch Lomond."

Qwilleran forgot his morning irritation with the publicity-seeking potter. "Here, let me help you," he offered.

Dan looked at Qwilleran warily, and his mouth dropped open. "Sorry if I said anything to get you riled up. I didn't know Maus would go blabbing it around."

"No harm done."

"It's your money. It's your business what you do with it, I guess."

"Forget it."

"Got a postcard today," Dan said. "Mailed from Cincinnati."

Qwilleran gulped twice before answering. "From your wife? How's everything?" He tried to speak casually. "Will she be back for the champagne party?"

"Guess not. She wants me to mail her summer duds to her in Miami."

"Miami!"

"Yep. Guess she's going to soak up some sunshine before she comes home. Do her some good. Give her a chance to think things over."

"No bad feeling, then?"

Dan scratched his head. "Husband and wife have to keep their identity, especially when they're artists. She'll get rid of that fuzzy feeling and come back, sassy as ever. We have our blowups; what couple doesn't?" He smiled his twisted smile, so much an imitation of Joy's smile that Qwilleran felt his flesh crawl. It was grotesque.

"It's a funny thing," Dan went on. "I used to ride her all the time about shedding hair all over the place. If it wasn't cat hairs floating around, it was her own—long ones—turning up in the clay and everywhere else. But you wanta know something? I kinda miss those aggravations when she's away. You ever been married?"

"I had a go at it once."

"Why don't you come up for a drink tomorrow night? Come on up to the loft."

"Thanks. I'll do that."

"Might give you a sneak preview of the exhibition.

Don't mind telling you I've come up with some dandies that'll rock 'em back on their heels. When you see your art critic, put a bug in his ear, if you know what I mean."

Qwilleran went up to Number Six, massaging his mustache as he climbed the stairs. The cats were alert and waiting for him.

"Well, what do you think of *that* development, Koko?" he said. "She's off to Miami."

"Yow!" Koko replied—ambiguously, Qwilleran thought.

"She hates Florida! She told us so, didn't she? And she's always been allergic to sunlight."

And then Qwilleran had a second thought. Perhaps his $750 check had financed a vacation with that food buyer—Fish, Ham, or whatever his name was—in the Sunshine State! Once again Qwilleran felt like a fool.

TEN

WHEN QWILLERAN'S ALARM went off on Saturday morning, it was still dark and chill, and he debated whether to fulfill his intentions or forget about the farmers' market and go back to sleep. Curiosity and a newsman's relish for an unfamiliar situation convinced him to get up.

He showered and dressed hastily and diced round steak for the cats, who were asleep in the big chair, stretched out in do-not-disturb postures.

By six-thirty Qwilleran was downstairs in the kitchen, where Robert Maus was breaking eggs into a bowl. "Hope you don't mind," Qwilleran said. "I've invited myself to go the farmers' market with you."

"Consider yourself more than welcome, to be sure," the attorney said. "Please be good enough to help yourself to orange juice and coffee. I am preparing . . . an omelet."

"Where's William?"

Maus took a deep breath before replying. "With

William, I regret to say, it is a point of honor to be late for any and all occasions."

He poured the beaten eggs into the omelet pan, shook it vigorously, stirred with a fork, folded the shimmering yellow creation, flipped it onto a warm plate, grated some white pepper over the top, and glazed it with butter.

It was the best omelet Qwilleran had ever tasted. With each tender, creamy mouthful he recalled the dry, brown, leathery imitations he had eaten in second-class restaurants. Maus prepared another omelet for himself and sat down at the table.

"I hate to see our friend William missing this good breakfast," said Qwilleran. "Maybe he overslept. Maybe I should hammer on his door."

He found William's room at the end of the kitchen corridor and knocked once, twice, then louder, without getting any response. He turned the knob gently and opened the door an inch or two. "William!" he shouted. "It's after six-thirty!" There was no sound from within. He peered into the room. The built-in bunk was empty, and the bedspread was neatly tucked under the mattress.

Qwilleran glanced around the room. The bathroom door stood open. He tried another door, which proved to be a small, untidy closet. The entire place was in mild disorder, with clothes and magazines scattered in all the wrong places.

He returned to the breakfast table. "Not there. His bed looks as if he hasn't slept in it, and the alarm clock hasn't been set. I took him out to dinner last night, and he was going to his mother's house afterward. Do you suppose he stayed there?"

"Basing an opinion on what I know about the relationship between William and his mother," said Maus, "I would . . . deem it more likely that he spent the night with the young lady to whom he appears to be . . . engaged. I suggest you wear boots this morning, Mr. Qwilleran. The market manufactures an exclusive brand of . . . mud, composed of wilted cabbage leaves, rotted tomatoes, crushed grapes, and an unidentifiable liquid that binds them together in a slimy black . . . amalgam."

The men started for the market in the attorney's old Mercedes, and as they circled the driveway, Qwilleran thought he saw the enormous tail fins of William's limousine protruding from the carport on the other side of the house.

"I think William's car is there," he remarked. "If he didn't come home last night, how did his car get back?"

"The ways of the young," said Maus, "are incomprehensible. I have ceased all attempts to understand their behavior."

It was true about the mud. A black ooze filled the gutters and splashed up over the sidewalks of the open-air market. There were several square blocks of open sheds where farmers and other vendors sold directly from their trucks. Rich and poor streamed through the cluttered aisles, carrying shopping bags, pushing baby buggies loaded with pots of geraniums, pulling red express wagons filled with produce, or maneuvering chrome-plated, rubber-tired shopping carts through the crowded aisles.

A pickpocket's heaven, Qwilleran thought.

There were women with rollers in their hair, children riding piggyback, distinguished old men in velvet-collared coats, Indian girls with tweed jackets over their filmy saris, teenagers wearing earphones, suburban housewives swaddled in fun furs, and more than the average number of immensely fat women.

Maus led the way between mountains of rhubarb and acres of fresh eggs, past the gallon jugs of honey, the whole pigs, bunches of sassafras, pillows filled with chicken feathers, carrots as big as baseball bats, white doves in cages, and purple cauliflower.

It was a nippy morning, and the vendors stamped their feet and warmed their hands over coke fires burning in oil drums. The smoke mingled with the aromas of apples, livestock, lilacs, and market mud. Qwilleran noticed a blind man with a white cane standing near the lilacs, sniffing and smiling.

Maus bought mushrooms, fern shoots, scallions, Florida corn, and California strawberries. It amazed the newsman to hear him haggling over the price of a turnip. "My dear woman, if you can afford to sell a dozen for three dollars, how can you—in all decency—ask thirty cents for one?" asked the man who served a ten-dollar bottle of wine with the jellied clams.

At one stall Maus selected a skinned rabbit, and Qwilleran turned away while the farmer wrapped the red, stiffened carcass in a sheet of newspaper and the white-furred relatives of the deceased looked on with reproach.

"Mrs. Marron, I must admit, makes an excellent hasenpfeffer," Maus explained. "She will prepare the . . . viands this weekend while I attend a gourmet conclave out of town . . . for which I happen to be the . . . master of ceremonies."

From the open-air market they went into the general market, a vast arena with hundreds of stalls under one roof and a soft carpet of sawdust underfoot. Hucksters with hoarse voices offered spiced salt belly, strudel dough, chocolate tortes, plaster figures of saints, quail eggs, voodoo potions, canned grape leaves, octopus, and perfumed floor wash guaranteed to bring good luck. A nickel-plated machine ground fresh peanut butter. A phonograph played harem music at a record stall. Maus bought snails and some Dutch mustard seed.

For a moment Qwilleran closed his eyes and tried to sort out the heady mix of smells: freshly ground coffee, strong cheese, garlic sausage, anise, dried codfish, incense. A wave of cheap perfume reached his nostrils, and he opened his eyes to see a Gypsy woman looking at him from a nearby stall. She smiled, and he blinked his eyes. She had Joy's smile, Joy's tiny figure, and Joy's long hair, but her face was a hundred years old. Her clothes were soiled, and her hair looked as if it had never been washed.

"Tell the fortune?"she invited.

Fascinated by this cruel caricature, Qwilleran nodded.

"You sit."

He sat on an upended beer case, and the woman sat opposite, shuffling a deck of dirty cards.

"How much?" he asked.

"Dollar. One dollar, yes?"

She laid out the cards in a cross and studied them. "I see water. You take long trip—boat—soon, yes?"

"Not very likely," Qwilleran said. "What else do you see?"

"Somebody sick. You get letter . . . I see money. Lotsa money. You like."

"Don't we all?"

"Young boy—your son? Some day great man. Big doctor."

"Where is my childhood sweetheart? Can you tell me that?"

"Hmmm . . . she far away—happy—lotsa children."

"You're phenomenal. You're a genius," Qwilleran grumbled. "Anything else?"

"I see water—so much water. You no like. Everybody wet."

Qwilleran escaped from the Gypsy's booth and caught up with his landlord. "Better fix the roof," he told him. "There's going to be another biblical-type flood." He shook himself, as if he might have picked up fleas.

When the two men carried their market purchases into the kitchen at Maus Haus, Mrs. Marron said to Qwilleran, "A man from the newspaper called. He said you should call him. Mr. Piper. Art Piper."

"Where've you been?" Arch Riker demanded when Qwilleran got him on the phone. "Out all night?"

"I've been to the farmers' market, getting material for a column, and I expect to collect time-and-a-half for getting up at an ungodly hour on my day off. What's on your mind?"

"I wish you'd help me out, Qwill. Would you drive to

Rattlesnake Lake to act as one of the judges in a contest?"

"Bathing beauties?"

"No. Cake-baking. It's the statewide thing sponsored by the John Stuart Flour Mills. They do a lot of advertising, and we promised we'd send one of the judges."

"Why can't the food editor do it?" Qwilleran snapped.

"She's in the hospital."

"Been eating her own cooking?"

"Qwill, you're crabby today. What's wrong with you?"

"To tell you the truth, Arch, I'd like to stick around here this weekend—to see what I can dig up. Joy's husband invited me in for a drink tonight. I don't want to talk about it on the phone, but you know what we discussed in the coffee shop."

"I know, Qwill, but we're in a jam. You can take some time off next week."

"Can't the women's department handle this contest?"

"They've got a lot of spring weddings to cover. You could make a nice weekend of it, take a company car and drive up this afternoon. You could have a nice dinner at the Rattlesnake Inn—they're famous for their food—and come back tomorrow night."

"They're famous for their bad food, not famous for their good food," Qwilleran objected. "Besides, how can I enjoy a dinner anywhere and stay on my diet? How can I judge a cake contest and lose any weight?"

"You'll figure something out. You're an old pro," said Riker.

"I'll make a deal with you," Qwilleran said after a moment's hesitation. "I'll go to Rattlesnake Lake if you'll send me Odd Bunsen on Monday to shoot pictures in the pottery."

"You think it's a story? We've done potteries before. They all look alike."

"It may not make a story, but I want an excuse to get

in there and prowl around." The newsman smoothed his mustache with his knuckles. "We've had another mysterious disappearance, Arch. This time it's the houseboy."

There was silence from Riker as he weighed the alternatives. "Well . . . I'll requisition a photographer, but I can't guarantee you'll get Bunsen."

"I don't want anyone else. It's got to be a nut like Bunsen."

At noon, when Qwilleran reported downstairs for lunch, he asked if anyone had seen William.

Hixie, who was busy chewing, shook her head.

Dan said, "Nope."

Rosemary remarked that it was unusual for William to miss market day.

Mrs. Marron said, "He was supposed to wax the floors today."

Charlotte Roop was engrossed in her crossword puzzle and said nothing.

Mrs. Marron was serving home-baked beans with brown bread and leftover ham, and Dan looked at the fare with distaste. "What's for dinner?" he demanded.

"Some nice roast chicken and wild rice."

"Chicken *again*? We just had it on Monday."

"And a nice coconut custard pie."

"I don't like coconut. It gets in my teeth," he said, making a sandwich of brown bread and ham.

"And tomorrow a nice rabbit stew," the housekeeper added.

"Ecch!"

"Mrs. Marron," Qwilleran interrupted, "these baked beans are delicious."

She gave him a grateful glance. "It's because I use an old bean pot. Forty years old, Mr. Maus says. It was made right here in the pottery, and it's signed on the bottom—H.M.H."

"That must have been about the time the sculptor was murdered," Qwilleran remarked.

"It was an accidental drowning," Miss Roop corrected him, looking up briefly from her puzzle.

"Nobody really believes that," said Hixie, and then she recited in a singsong voice:

"A potty young sculptor, Mort Mellon,
Fell in love with a pottress named Helen,
But the pottery gods frowned
And he promptly got drowned.
Who pushed him the potters ain't tellin'."

Miss Roop lifted her chin. "That's very disrespectful, Miss Rice."

"Who cares?" Hixie retorted. "They're all dead."

"Mr. Maus would not like it, if he were here."

"But he's not here. By now he's halfway to Miami."

"*Miami*?" Qwilleran echoed.

Mrs. Marron brought him some more ham, which he regretfully declined, although he accepted some scraps for his roommates. "By the way," he said to her, "I'm going to be out of town overnight. Would you be good enough to feed my cats tomorrow morning?"

"I don't know much about cats," she said. "Is there anything special I have to do?"

"Just dice some meat for them and give them fresh water. And be absolutely sure they don't get out of the apartment." To the others at the table he said, "I have an assignment at Rattlesnake Lake. Dan, I'll have to take a rain check on your invitation, but we might be lucky enough to get a photographer here on Monday."

Dan grunted and nodded.

Qwilleran went on: "I hate the thought of the long drive up to the lake in a company car. The *Fluxion* seems to have bought a whole fleet of lemons."

A soft voice at his left said, "Would you like company? I'd be happy to go along for the ride. You could drive my car." The newsman turned and looked into the eyes of Rosemary Whiting—the quiet one, the thoughtful one who had brought the cats a ball of yarn. Her brown eyes were filled with an expression he could not immediately identify. He had not realized she was so attractive—her eyes dancing with health, her skin like whipped cream, her dark hair glossy.

Having hesitated too long, he said hurriedly, "Sure! Sure! I'd be grateful for your company. If we leave right after lunch, we'll have time for a leisurely drive and a good dinner at the inn. I have to judge a contest, but it doesn't take place until tomorrow afternoon, so we can sleep late tomorrow and stop somewhere for a bite to eat on the way home."

Miss Roop went on working her crossword puzzle with her lips frozen in a thin, straight line.

ELEVEN

"KOKO DIDN'T WANT me to make this trip," Qwilleran told Rosemary, as they drove away from Maus Haus in her dark blue compact. "As soon as I got out my luggage, he started to scold."

He glanced at his passenger. At Maus Haus he had guessed her age to be about thirty, but seeing her in daylight he increased his estimate to forty—a young forty.

"You look wonderful," he said. "That wheat germ you sprinkle on everything must agree with you. How long have you had your health food shop?"

"Two years," she said. "After my husband died, I sold the house and moved downtown and invested the money in the business."

"Any children?"

"Two sons. They're both doctors."

Qwilleran sneaked another look at his passenger and did some simple arithmetic. Forty-five? Fifty?"

"Tell me," Rosemary said. "What brought you to Maus Haus?"

He told her about his new assignment, the invitation to attend a gourmet dinner given by Robert Maus, and his unexpected reunion with Joy Graham, an old friend.

She said, "I guessed it was more than a casual acquaintance."

"You're very discerning. Joy and I were planning to marry at one time, many years ago." He jammed on the brakes. "Sorry," he apologized. "Did you see that stupid cat? It strolled casually across the highway, and as soon as it reached safety, it ran like the devil."

"I hope you didn't think I was awfully bold to invite myself on this trip, Mr. Qwilleran."

"Not at all. I'm delighted. I wish I'd thought of it first. And please call me Qwill. I'm certainly not going to call you Mrs. Whiting all weekend."

"I had a reason for wanting to come. There's something I want to discuss with you, but not right now. I'd like to enjoy the scenery."

As they drove through the countryside, Rosemary observed and remarked about every cider mill, gravel pit, corn crib, herd of cattle, stone barn, and split-rail fence. She had a pleasant voice, and Qwilleran found her company relaxing. By the time they reached Rattlesnake Inn, he was experiencing a comfortable contentment. She remarked that it would be nice if they could have adjoining rooms. It was going to be a good weekend, he told himself.

The inn was a rickety frame structure that should have burned down half a century before. Weeping willows drooped over the edge of the lake, and canoes glided over its glassy surface. Before dinner Qwilleran rented a flat-bottomed boat and rowed Rosemary across the lake and back. During the cocktail hour they danced—Qwilleran's nameless, formless, ageless dance step that he had invented twenty-five years before and had not bothered to update.

"I think I'll celebrate," he said. "I'm going off my diet tonight."

Although Rattlesnake Inn was not celebrated for the

quality of its food, it was unsurpassed in terms of quantity. The hors d'oeuvre table presented thirty different appetizers, all of them mashed up and flavored with the same pickle juice. The menu offered a choice of ten steaks, all uniformly tender, expensive, and flavorless. The shrimp cocktails were huge and leathery. An impressive assortment of rolls, biscuits, and muffins came to the table in bun-warmers that were ice cold. The baked potatoes wore foil jackets firmly glued to the skin, except for minute fragments of foil mashed into the interior. The Rattlesnake Inn served asparagus that tasted like Brussels sprouts and spinach that tasted like old dishrags. Individual wooden salad bowls, twelve inches in diameter and rancid with age, were heaped with anemic lettuce and wedges of synthetic tomato. But the specialty of the house was the dessert buffet with twenty-seven cream pies made from instant vanilla pudding.

Yet, such was the magic of the occasion that neither Qwilleran nor Rosemary thought to complain about the food.

While they were lingering over cups of what the Rattlesnake Inn called coffee, Rosemary came to the point. "I want to talk to you about William," she said. "We've become good friends. A young man needs an older woman for a confidante—not his mother. Don't you agree?"

Qwilleran nodded.

"William has some good qualities. He lacks direction, but I have always been confident that he will find himself eventually. I know he thinks highly of you, and that's why I'm telling you this . . . I'm worried about him. I'm alarmed at his absence."

Qwilleran stroked his mustache. "What's the reason for your alarm?"

"He came home about eleven o'clock last night, after going to see his mother, and he stopped in my apartment and told me a few things."

"What kind of things?"

"Well, he's a very inquisitive person . . ."

"That I know."

"And he's been questioning some of the recent incidents at Maus Haus. He thinks there is more to them than meets the eye."

"Did he mention anything specifically?"

"He told me he thought he 'had something' on Dan Graham and he was going to investigate. He fancies himself a detective, you know, and he reads all those crime stories. I told him not to meddle."

"You have no idea what sort of malfeasance he suspected?"

"No, he just said he was going to visit Dan last night and sponge a nightcap; he thought he might come up with some evidence."

"Did he go?"

"As far as I know. And this morning . . ."

"No William," said Qwilleran. "I went looking for him, and his bed hadn't been slept in, I'm sure of that."

"And yet his car is in the carport . . . I don't know . . . No one else seems to be concerned. Mr. Maus says he's impetuous. Mrs. Marron says he's unreliable. What do you think, Qwill?"

"If he isn't there when we get home tomorrow night, we'll make some inquiries. Do you know how to get in touch with his mother?"

"She's in the phone book, I suppose. William also has a fiancée—or whatever."

"Do you think he might have gone off somewhere with her? Do we know who she is or where to reach her?"

Rosemary shook her head, and they both fell silent. After a while Qwilleran said, "I've been doing a little worrying myself. About Joy Graham. Was she interested in that food buyer? Would she go to Miami to be with him?"

"Mr. Hamilton? I don't think so. She has an exhibition coming up, and she's terribly dedicated to her art."

"Dan said he got a postcard, and she's on her way to

Miami; she wants her summer clothes shipped down there. She happened to tell me she hates Florida, so I don't know what to believe. How do you size up her husband, Rosemary?"

"I'm sorry, but I've never liked that man, and I'm sure the others feel the same way. Haven't you noticed the chill that falls on the conversation whenever Dan opens his mouth?"

"You know about the nasty situation at the Golden Lamb Chop," Qwilleran said. "Did that start after the Grahams arrived at Maus Haus?"

"I believe it did."

"Do you suppose Dan could be responsible? He's the jealous type."

"I really don't think there's anything going on between Joy and Max. They're too friendly in public. If they were having an affair, they'd be carefully ignoring each other at the dinner table. Besides, I think Max is too fastidious to have affairs. He never even shakes hands with anyone, male or female." She stopped to giggle. "William says Max is the kind who dries his toothbrush with a hair blower."

Qwilleran pulled on his pipe, and Rosemary sipped the stuff in her coffee cup. After a while she said, "Did it ever occur to you that Mr. Maus is a lonely and unhappy man?"

"I don't know why he should be," said Qwilleran. "He has his French knives and his eight-burner stove."

"You're not being serious," she chided. "His wife is dead, you know, and his heart isn't in the law business; he should be running a fine restaurant. On Tuesday night, after I'd had dinner at my son's house, I came home after midnight and saw a light in the kitchen, so I went in to investigate. There was Mr. Maus sitting at the table with his head in his hands. He was holding a piece of raw meat on his eye."

"Filet mignon, of course."

"All right. I won't tell you the rest of it."

"Please. I'm sorry."

"Well, he told me he'd been sitting on the bench down by the river and tripped on the boardwalk when he started to leave. Don't you think that's rather sad—sitting down by the river all alone?"

"He had a different explanation for me," Qwilleran said. "Would you like to dance? I'm a sad, lonely, unhappy man, too."

They danced slowly and thoughtfully, and Qwilleran was thinking of suggesting a walk in the moonlight when he was suddenly overcome by complete exhaustion. His shoulders sagged; his face felt drawn. He had been up since dawn, tramping around the farmers' market, and then there had been the long drive, followed by boating (he hadn't rowed a boat for fifteen years) and then dancing and a large meal . . .

"Are you tired?" Rosemary asked. "You've had a long day. Why don't we go upstairs?"

Qwilleran agreed gratefully.

"Would you like me to massage your neck and shoulders?" she asked. "It will relax you, and you'll sleep beautifully. But first a hot bath, so you won't have sore muscles after all that rowing."

She drew the bath for him, coloring the water lettuce green with mineral salts, and after he had soaked the prescribed twenty minutes, she produced a bottle of lotion that smelled faintly of cucumber. The soothing massage, the aromatic lotion, and Rosemary's murmured phrases that he only half heard made him drowsy. He felt—he wondered—he wanted to say—but he was so relaxed . . . so sleepy . . . perhaps tomorrow . . .

It was noon when Qwilleran awoke on Sunday and learned that Rosemary had been up since seven and had hiked around the lake. They lunched hurriedly and reported to the ballroom for the cake-judging, only to discover that the plans had been changed. The judging had taken place before noon to accommodate the television crews. However, Qwilleran was towed around the ballroom by a public relations person to meet the beaming winners.

He congratulated the grandmotherly creator of the inside-out marble mocha whipped cream cake, the vivacious young matron with her brazil nut caramel angel cake, the delicate young man who was so proud of his sour cream chocolate velvet icebox cake, and finally the winner in the teenage class. She was a tiny girl with long straight hair and a wistful smile, and she had concocted a psychedelic cake. Qwilleran stared at the conglomeration of chocolate, nuts, marshmallows, strawberries, and coconut—the banana split cake of twenty-five years ago. He looked at the girl and saw Joy.

"Let's get out of here," he whispered to Rosemary. "I'm seeing ghosts."

They drove home in the late evening—both of them relaxed and content to talk or not to talk as the mood prevailed—and it was midnight when they walked into the Great Hall at Maus Haus.

"When can I take you out to dinner again?" he asked Rosemary. "How about Tuesday evening?"

"I'd love to," she said, "but I have to attend a recital. One of my grandsons is playing the violin."

"You have a *grandson*?"

"I have three grandchildren."

"I can't believe you're a grandmother! This violinist must be an infant prodigy."

"He's twelve," said Rosemary as they started to climb the stairs. "He's the youngest. The other two are in college."

Qwilleran gazed at the grandmother-of-three with admiration. "You'd better get me some of that wheat germ," he said. She smiled sweetly and triumphantly, and Qwilleran dropped the suitcases and kissed her.

At that moment they heard an outcry. Mrs. Marron came running from the kitchen corridor. She burst into tears.

Rosemary ran downstairs and put an arm around the housekeeper. "What is it, Mrs. Marron? What's wrong?"

"Something—something terrible," the woman

wailed. "I don't know how to tell you."

Qwilleran hurried down the stairs. "Is it William? What's happened?"

Mrs. Marron gave him a terrified glance and launched another torrent of tears. "It's the cats!" she wailed. "They took sick."

"*What*!" Qwilleran started to bolt up the stairs three at a time but suddenly stopped. "Where are they?"

Mrs. Marron groaned. "They were—they were taken away."

"Where?" he demanded. "To the vet? Which one? To the hospital?"

She shook her head and covered her face with her hands. "I called . . . I called the . . . Sanitation Department. They're dead!"

"*Dead*! They can't be! *Both* of them? They were perfectly all right. What happened?"

The housekeeper was too shaken to answer. She could only moan.

"Were they poisoned? They must have been poisoned! Who went near them?" He took Mrs. Marron by the shoulders and shook her. "Who got into my apartment? What did you feed them?"

She moved her head miserably from side to side.

"By God!" Qwilleran said, "If it was poison, I'll kill the one who did it!"

TWELVE

QWILLERAN PACED THE floor of his apartment. Rosemary had offered to sit with him, but he had sent her away.

"My God! The Sanitation Department!" he said aloud, slapping his forehead with the palm of his hand. "Not even a chance to—I could have—at least I could have buried them with some kind of dignity." He stopped, aware that he was talking to the four walls. He was accustomed to an audience. They had been such attentive listeners, such satisfactory companions, always ready to supply encouragement, entertainment, or solace, depending on his mood, which they had been able to sense unerringly. And now they were gone. He could not come to terms with the idea.

"The Sanitation Department!" he said again with a groan. Now he remembered: Koko had not wanted him to take the weekend trip. Perhaps the cat had an intimation of danger. The thought made Qwilleran's grief all the more painful. His hands were clenched, his forehead damp. He was ready to destroy the beast who had destroyed those two innocent creatures. But where could he pin the blame? And how could he prove anything? Without the two small bodies he could never prove poison. But someone must have entered his apartment during his absence. Who? The only tenants in the house over the weekend, besides Mrs. Marron, were Max Sorrel, Charlotte Roop, Hixie, and Dan Graham. And perhaps William, if he had returned.

Qwilleran picked up the cats' empty food plate and sniffed it. He took a sip from their water dish and spit it out. He smelled nothing unusual, tasted nothing suspicious. But he heard footsteps coming up the stairs. It would be Maus, he decided, returning from his weekend in Miami.

Qwilleran threw open his door and stepped into the hall to confront his landlord. It was not Maus; it was Max Sorrel.

"Man, what's wrong with you?" Sorrel said. "You look like you've got the d.t.'s."

"Did you hear what happened to my cats?" Qwilleran bellowed. "I went away overnight, and they took sick and died. At least, that's the story I got."

"Damn shame! I know how you felt about those little monkeys."

"I'll tell you one thing! I'm not satisfied with the explanation. I think they were poisoned! And whoever did it is going to regret it!"

Sorrel shook his head. "I don't know. I think there's a jinx on this house. First the housekeeper and then me and then—"

"What do you mean? What about the housekeeper?" Qwilleran demanded.

"Tragic! Really tragic! Her grandson came to visit—little kid *this high*—and he fell in the river. Loose board in the boardwalk, they think . . . Look, Qwilleran, you need a slug of whiskey. Come on in and have a shot."

"No, thanks," said Qwilleran wearily. "I've got to work it out in my own way."

He returned to Number Six and gazed at the emptiness. He wanted to move out. He would leave tomorrow. Go to a hotel. He made note of the things he would no longer need: the harness and leash hanging on the back of a chair; the blue cushion; the brush he had bought and forgotten to use; the cats' commode in the bathroom with the gravel neatly scratched into one corner. They had been so meticulous about their housekeeping. Qwilleran's eyes grew moist.

Knowing he would be unable to sleep, he sat down at his typewriter to turn out a column for the paper—a requiem for two lost friends. Putting it down on paper would relieve the pain, he knew. Now would be the time to reveal to the public Koko's remarkable capabilities. He had solved three mysteries—homicide cases. He was probably the only cat in the country who owned a press card signed by the chief of police. Qwilleran rested his hands on the typewriter keys and wondered how to start, and as his mind swam in an ocean of words—none of them adequate—his eyes fell on the sheet of paper in the machine. There were two letters typed there: pb.

The newsman felt a chill in the roots of his mustache: *poisoned beef*!

Just then he heard a distant cry. He listened sharply. It sounded like a child's cry. He thought of the drowned boy and shuddered. The cry came again, louder, and in the darkness outside the window there was a pale form hovering. Qwilleran rubbed his eyes and stared in disbelief. There was a scratching at the window.

"Koko!" the man yelled, yanking open the casement.

The cat hopped down onto the desk, followed by Yum Yum, both of them blinking at the lamplight. They made no sign of greeting but jumped to the floor and trotted to the kitchen, looking for their dinner plate. Avidly they lapped up water from their bowl.

"You're starved!" Qwilleran said. "How long have you been out there? . . . Sanitation Department! What's wrong with that woman? She was hallucinating!" He hurried to open a can of red salmon and watched them as they gobbled it. There was no observation of feline protocol this time, no nonsense about males before females; Yum Yum fought for her share.

Now Qwilleran dropped into his armchair, feeling an overwhelming fatigue. The cats finished eating, washed their faces, and then climbed into his lap together—something they had never done before. Their feet and tails were cold. They crawled up Qwilleran's chest and lay on their bellies, side by side, looking into his face. Their eyes were large and anxious.

He hugged them both. He hugged Yum Yum tightly because he remembered how—in his first frenzied reaction to the bad news—his concern had been chiefly for Koko. He reproached himself now. He cherished them both equally, and if he valued Koko for his special talents, he also valued Yum Yum for her winning ways and the heartbreaking way she looked at him with slightly crossed eyes. In apology he hugged her more tightly.

To Koko he said, "And I don't care if you never solve another case."

There was a definite odor about the cats. He sniffed their fur. It smelled earthy.

After a while they warmed their extremities and felt contented enough to purr, and eventually they dozed, still huddled on Qwilleran's chest. He fell asleep himself and woke at daybreak, his shoulders stiff and his neck virtually paralyzed. The cats had moved to more comfortable berths elsewhere.

At first he had difficulty convincing himself that the panic of the night before had not been a nightmare, but as he took a hot shower he remembered the pleasures of the weekend as well as the pain he had felt upon arriving home. On his way down to breakfast he slipped a note under Rosemary's door: "False alarm! Cats are home. Just wandered away. Mrs. M. is crazy."

In the kitchen he found only Hixie, scrambling eggs and toasting split pecan rolls.

"Have you heard the news?" she asked with glee.

"Mickey Maus is in Cuba. His plane was hijacked. And Mrs. Marron has quit, so we're all on our own this morning."

"She's quit her job?"

"She left a note on the kitchen table saying she couldn't stay after what happened this weekend. What happened? Did she get raped or something?"

"I don't know exactly what happened or how," Qwilleran said, "but she told a fib. I don't know why, but she told me the cats got sick and died. Actually they'd climbed out the window, and they came home after midnight."

"She was acting funny all day yesterday," Hixie said. "Why would she say they were dead?"

"Do you know how to get in touch with her? I'd like to tell her to come back."

"She has a married daughter somewhere in town . . . Oh, brother! This was the weekend that shouldn't! Yesterday the hot water heater conked out; Mickey Maus was out of town; a delegation from the tennis club came over with a complaint; William never showed up; Max was working; Charlotte had the pip; so little me had to cope with everything, as if I didn't have enough troubles of my own. Want some scrambled eggs?"

After breakfast Qwilleran telephoned Mrs. Marron's daughter. "Tell her everything is all right. Tell her the cats have come back. Ask her if she'll come to the phone and speak to Mr. Qwilleran."

After some delay, Mrs. Marron came on the line, whimpering.

"Don't worry about anything," Qwilleran reassured her. "There's no harm done, except that you gave me some anxious moments. The cats apparently got out on the roof. Did you open the window when you cleaned my room Saturday?"

"Just for a minute, when I shook the dustmop. They were asleep on that blue cushion. I looked to see."

"Perhaps you didn't latch the window completely; Koko is expert at opening latches if they're halfway loose. But why did you invent that story about the Sanitation Department?"

Mrs. Marron was silent, except for moist sniffing.

"I'm not angry, Mrs. Marron. I just want to know why."

"I knew they had gone. When I went in to feed them on Sunday morning, I couldn't find them. I thought—I thought they'd been snatched. You know what Mr. Graham always says—"

"But why did you tell me they were dead?"

"I thought—I thought it would be better for you to—think they were dead than not to know." She started to sob. "My little Nicky, my grandson, he was missing for two weeks before they found him. It's terrible not to know."

Gently Qwilleran said, "You must come back, Mrs. Marron. We all need you. Will you come back?"

"Do you mean it?"

"Yes, I mean it sincerely. Hurry back before Mr. Maus returns, and we won't say a word about the incident."

Before leaving for the office, Qwilleran groomed the cats' fur with the new brush. Koko took a fiendish delight in the procedure—arching his back, craning his neck, gargling throaty comments of appreciation. Then he flopped down on his side and made swimming motions.

"You've got a pretty good sidestroke," Qwilleran said. "We may get you on the Olympic team."

Yum Yum, however, had to be chased around the apartment for five minutes before she would submit to the brushing process, which she obviously adored.

"Typical female," Qwilleran muttered, breathing heavily after the chase.

Their fur still smelled strongly of something. Was it clay? Had they been in the Grahams' clay room? They could have gone out the window, around the ledge, and through another window. Then Mrs. Marron, coming in to feed them, had latched the casement, locking them out. Had they climbed onto the ledge to look for pigeons? Or did Koko have a reason for wanting to snoop in the pottery? Qwilleran felt an uneasiness in the roots of his mustache.

He opened the window to inspect the ledge. He moved the desk and gave a jump, hoisting himself across the high sill. Leaning far out, teetering across the sill, he could see the entire length of the ledge as it passed under the high windows of the kiln room and the large windows of a room beyond, probably the Grahams' loft apartment. But when he tried to wriggle back into the apartment, the window seemed to have shrunk. Inside the room his legs kicked ineffectually, while the bulk of his weight was outside.

Koko, fascinated by the spectacle of half a man where there should have been a whole one, leaped to the desk and howled.

"Don't yell at me! Call for help!" Quilleran shouted over his shoulder, but Koko only came closer and howled in the vicinity of Qwilleran's hip pocket.

"What are you doing up there?" came a woman's voice from below. Hixie was on her way to the garage.

"I'm stuck, dammit! Come up and give me a toehold."

He continued to teeter on the fulcrum of the sill while Hixie ran indoors, ran upstairs to Number Six, ran downstairs to get the key from the kitchen, and ran upstairs again. After a few minutes of pulling, pushing, bracing, squeezing, and grunting—with Hixie squealing and the cats yowling—Qwilleran was dislodged. He thanked her gruffly.

"Would you like to go to a meeting with me tomorrow night?" she asked. "It's the dinner meeting of the Friendly Fatties. . . . Nothing personal, of course," she added.

Qwilleran mumbled that he might consider it.

"So this is the famous Siamese pussycat," she said on her way out. "*Bon jour*, Koko."

"*Yaeioux*," said Koko, replying in French.

Qwilleran went to his office to write a routine piece about the cake-baking contest for the second edition and to get a confirmation on his photo requisition. The assignment was on the board for five o'clock, earmarked for Bunsen, and Qwilleran telephoned Dan Graham to alert him.

"Swell! That's swell!" said Dan. "Didn't think you'd be able to swing it. That's a real break. Don't mind telling you I appreciate it. I'd like to do something for you. How about a bottle? Do you like bourbon? What does your photographer drink?"

"Forget the payola," Qwilleran said. "The story may never get in the paper. All we can do is write it and shoot the pictures and pray a lot." And then he added, "Just remembered, I have some friends on the Miami papers, including an art critic who might like to meet Joy while she's there. Could you give me her address?"

"In Miami? I don't know. She didn't know where she'd be holing up."

"How are you mailing her summer clothes, then?"

"To General Delivery," said Dan.

Qwilleran waited in the office for the first edition. He wanted to see how they were handling his new column. *Prandial Musings* appeared in thumb position on the op-ed page—a good spot!—with a photograph of the mustached author looking grimly pleased.

"Who thought of the name for my column?" he grumbled to Arch Riker. "It sounds like gastric burbulance. Ninety percent of our readers won't know what it means."

"Make that ninety-eight percent," said Arch.

"It sounds as if the byline should be Addison and Steele."

"The boss wanted something dignified," the feature editor explained. "Would you rather call it *Swill with Qwill*? That title did cross my mind . . . How was your weekend?"

"Not bad. Not bad at all. The cats gave me a helluva scare when I got home, but it turned out all right."

"Any news from Joy?"

Qwilleran related Dan's story about the alleged postcard and Joy's alleged plans to go to Miami. "And we've had another disappearance," he said. "Now the houseboy has vanished."

He went to his desk and telephoned the Penniman Art School. William, who should have been in freehand drawing that hour, was absent, according to the registrar's office. The newsman then looked up Vitello in the phone book and called the only one listed; it was a tea-leaf reading salon and the proprietor had never heard of William. Blowing into his mustache, as he did when his course was not clear, Qwilleran ambled out of the office. He was passing the receptionist's desk when a girl who was waiting there touched his sleeve.

"Are you Mr. Qwilleran?" she asked. "I recognized you from your picture. I'm a friend of William Vitello. May I talk to you?" She was a serious young girl, wearing serious glasses and unflattering clothes. The ragbag look, Qwilleran thought. She's an art student, he decided.

"Sure," he said. "Let's sit down over here." He led the way into one of the cubicles where reporters patiently listened to the irate readers, petitioners, publicity-seekers, and certifiable cranks who daily swarmed into the *Fluxion* editorial offices. "Have you seen William lately?" he asked the girl.

"No. That's what I wanted to talk about," she said. "We had a date Saturday night, but he never showed up. Never even called. Sunday I phoned Maus Haus, and he wasn't there. Some woman answered the phone, but she wasn't very coherent. Today he's not in school."

"Did you get in touch with his mother?"

"She hasn't heard from him since he took her a birthday present Friday night. I don't know what I should do. I thought of you because William talked about you a lot. What do you think I should do?"

"William is impetuous. He might have decided to take a trip somewhere."

"He wouldn't go without telling me, Mr. Qwilleran. We're very close. We even have a joint bank account."

The newsman propped one elbow on the arm of the chair and combed his mustache with his fingertips. "Did he ever discuss the situation at Maus Haus?"

"Oh, he's always talking about that weird place. He says it's full of characters."

"Did he ever mention Dan Graham?"

The girl nodded, giving Qwilleran a glance from the corner of her eye.

"Anything you want to tell me is confidential," he assured her.

"Well, I really didn't take him seriously. He said he was spying on Mr. Graham. He said he was going to dig up some dirt. I thought he was just kidding, or showing off. Billy likes to read spy stories, and he gets ideas."

"Do you know what kind of irregularity he suspected? Was it a morals situation?"

"You mean—like sex?" The girl bit her thumbnail as she considered that possibility. "Well, maybe. But the main story had something to do with the way Mr. Graham was running the pottery. Something fishy was going on in the pottery, Billy said."

"When did he last mention this?"

"Friday night. He phoned me after he had dinner with you."

"Did he mention any specific detail about the pottery operation? Think hard."

The girl frowned. "Only that . . . he said he thought Mr. Graham was going to blow a whole load of pots."

"Destroy them?"

"Billy said he was firing the kiln wrong and the whole load would blow. He couldn't understand it, because Mr. Graham is supposed to be a good fireman . . . I'm not much help, am I?"

"I'll be able to answer that later," Qwilleran told her. "Wait another forty-eight hours, and if William doesn't turn up, you'd better notify Missing Persons, or have his mother do it. And another thing: You might check your joint bank account for sizable withdrawals."

"Yes, I'll do that, Mr. Qwilleran. Thank you so much, Mr. Qwilleran." Her wide eyes were magnified through the lenses of her glasses. "Only . . . all we've got in the bank is eighteen dollars."

THIRTEEN

QWILLERAN RETURNED TO Maus Haus on the River Road bus, pondering the pieces of the puzzle: two missing persons, a drowned child, a slandered restaurateur, a lost cat, a black eye, a scream in the night. Too many pieces were missing.

Up in Number Six the cats were snoozing on the blue cushion. They had been busy, however, and several pictures were tilted. Qwilleran automatically straightened them, a chore to which he had become accustomed. The cats had to have their fun, he rationalized. Cooped up in a one-room apartment, they had to use ingenuity to amuse themselves, and Koko found a peculiar satisfaction in scraping his jaw on the sharp corners of a picture frame. Qwilleran straightened two engravings of bridges over the Seine, a Cape Cod watercolor, and a small oil painting of a beach scene on the Riviera. In the far corner an Art Nouveau print had been tilted so violently that it was hanging sideways. As he rectified the situation, he noticed a patch on the wall.

It was a metal patch, painted to match the stucco walls. He touched it, and it moved from side to side, pivoting on a tiny screw. Small arcs scratched in the wall paint indicated that the patch had been swung aside before, perhaps recently. Qwilleran swung it all the way around and discovered what it was concealing: a deep hole in the wall.

Leaning across the bookcase, he peered through the opening and looked down into the two-story kiln room behind his own apartment. The lights were turned on, and Qwilleran could see a central table with a collection of vases in brilliant blues, greens, and reds. Shifting his position to the left, he could see two of the kilns. Shifting to the right, he saw Dan Graham sitting at a small side table, copying from a loose-leaf notebook into a large ledger.

Qwilleran closed the peephole and replaced the picture, asking himself questions: What was its purpose? Did William know about it? Mrs. Marron said he had washed the walls recently. Had William been spying on Dan from this vantage point?

The telephone rang, and Odd Bunsen was on the line. "Say, what's the assignment you've got on the board for five o'clock? It sounds like a sizable job. When do I get to eat?"

"You can have dinner here," Qwilleran said, "and shoot the pictures afterward. The food here is great!"

"The requisition says two-five-five-five River Road. What is that place, anyway?"

"It's an old pottery, now a gourmet boarding house."

"Sure, I know the place. There were a couple of murders there. We keep running stories on them. Any special equipment I should bring?"

"Bring everything," Qwilleran advised. He lowered his voice with a glance in the direction of the peephole. "I want you to put on a good show. Bring lots of lights. I'll explain when you get here."

Qwilleran went downstairs to tell Mrs. Marron there would be an extra guest for dinner. She was in the Great Hall, nervously setting the dinner table, which had been moved under the balcony to make room for the pottery exhibit.

"I don't know what to do," she was whimpering. "They said they'd do a demonstration dinner, but I don't know how they want it set up. Nobody told me. Nobody's here."

"What's a demonstration dinner?" Qwilleran asked.

"Everybody cooks something at the table. Mr. Sorrel, he's making the steak. Mrs. Whiting, she's making the soup. Miss Roop, she's—"

"Have you seen William?"

"No, sir, and he was supposed to clean the stove—"

"Any news from Mr. Maus?"

"No, sir. Nobody knows when he'll be back . . . You're not going to tell him, are you? You said you wouldn't tell him."

"We're going to forget the whole matter," Qwilleran assured her. "Stop worrying about it, Mrs. Marron."

Tears came to her dull eyes, and she rubbed them away with the back of her hand. "Everybody is so good to me here. I try not to make mistakes, but I can't get little Nicky off my mind, and I don't sleep nights."

"We all understand what you've been through, but you must pull yourself together."

"Yes, sir." The housekeeper stopped her nervous puttering and turned to face him. "Mr. Qwilleran," she said hesitantly, "I heard something else in the night."

"What do you mean?"

"Saturday night, when I couldn't sleep, I was just lying there, worrying, and I heard a noise."

"What kind of noise?"

"Outside my window. Somebody coming down the fire escape."

"The one at the back of the house?"

"Yes, sir. My room is on the river side."

"Did you see anything?"

"No, sir. I got up and peeked out the window, but it was so dark. All I could see was somebody crossing the grass."

"Hmmm," Qwilleran mused. "Did you recognize the person?"

"No, sir. But I think it was a man. He was carrying a heavy load of something."

"What kind of load?"

"Like a big sack."

"How big?"

"This big!" The housekeeper spread her arms wide. "He was carrying it down to the river. When he got beyond the bushes, I couldn't see him anymore. But I *heard* it."

"What did you hear?"

"A big splash."

"And what happened then?"

"He came back."

"Did you get a look at his face then?"

"No, sir. There wasn't any light at the back of the building—just the bright lights across the river. But I could see him moving across the grass, and then I heard him going up the fire escape again."

"Is that the one that leads to the Grahams' loft?"

"Yes, sir."

"What time did this happen?"

"It was very late. Maybe four o'clock." The housekeeper looked at him hopefully, waiting for his approval.

Qwilleran studied her face briefly. "If it was Mr. Graham, there was probably some logical explanation. Think nothing of it."

"Yes, sir."

He went upstairs wondering: Did she really see Dan Graham dropping a sack in the river? She made up a story once before, and she could do it again. Perhaps she thinks I'm the kind that drools over mysteries, and she's trying to please me. And why all that yes-sir, no-sir business all of a sudden?

In his apartment Qwilleran's eye went first to the Art Nouveau print over the bookcase, and it gave him an idea. A few months before, he had interviewed a commercial potter who specialized in contemporary figurines, and now he telephoned him.

"This may sound like a crazy question," he told the potter, "but I'm trying my hand at writing a novel—kind of a Gothic thriller about skulduggery in a pottery. Would it be too farfetched to have a peephole in a wall overlooking the kiln room?"

"So the firing operation could be observed?"

"Yes. Something like that."

"Not a bad idea at all. I once suspected an employee of sabotaging my work, and I had to set up an expensive surveillance system. A simple peephole might have saved me a lot of money. Why didn't I think of that? All potters are professional voyeurs, you know. We're always looking through the spyholes in the kilns, and I can't pass a knothole in a board fence without taking a peek."

Odd Bunsen arrived at Maus Haus at five o'clock, and Qwilleran invited him to Number Six for a drink.

"Hey, you're getting taller," the photographer said. "It couldn't be thinner."

"I've lost seven pounds," Qwilleran boasted, unaware that three of them had been contributed in the beginning by Koko.

"Where are those crazy cats? Hiding?"

"Asleep on the shelves, behind the books."

Bunsen flopped in the big lounge chair, propped his feet on the ottoman, lit a cigar, and accepted a glass of something ninety-proof. "I wish the boss could see me now. Do you realize the *Fluxion* is paying me for this?"

"The work will come later." Qwilleran went to the peephole and checked the metal patch.

"What kind of hanky-panky did you have in mind?"

"Keep your voice down," Qwilleran advised. "If possible."

"Are you telling me I'm a loudmouth?"

"To put it tactfully . . . yes."

"What's the assignment all about? Don't keep me in suspense."

The newsman sat down and lit his pipe. "Ostensibly you'll be taking pictures for a layout on Dan Graham, who runs the pottery."

"But without any film in the camera?"

"We might use one or two pictures, but I want you to keep the camera clicking all over the place. I'd also like an excuse to get Koko into the pottery, but I don't want to suggest it myself." He groomed his mustache with his pipe stem.

Bunsen recognized the gesture. "Not another crime! Not again!"

"Lower your voice," Qwilleran said with a frown. "While you're preparing to shoot pictures, I want to browse around the premises, so take a lot of time doing it."

"You got the right man," said Bunsen. "I can set up a tripod slower than any other photographer in the business."

Later, at the dinner table, everyone liked the *Fluxion* photographer. Bunsen had a way of taking over a social occasion, bursting on the scene with his loud voice and jovial manner and stale jokes, jollying the women, kidding the men. Rosemary smiled at him, Hixie giggled, and even Charlotte Roop was fascinated when he called her a doll-baby. Max Sorrel invited Bunsen to bring his wife to dinner at the Golden Lamb Chop some evening. Dan Graham had not yet arrived.

For the first course Rosemary stood at the head of the table and demonstrated a sixty-second cold soup involving yogurt, cucumbers, dill, and raisins.

"Best soup I ever tasted!" Bunsen announced.

Dan Graham, arriving at the table late, was greeted coolly by the Maus Haus regulars, but the photographer jumped up and pumped his hand, and the potter glowed with suppressed excitement. He had had a haircut, and his shabby clothes were neater than usual.

Sorrel sautéed steak *au poivre*, which was served with Mrs. Marron's potato puffs and asparagus garnished with pimiento strips.

Then Charlotte Roop demonstrated the tossing of a salad. "Dry the greens carefully on a linen towel," she said. "Be careful not to bruise the leaves. Tear them apart tenderly . . . And now the dressing. I add a little Dijon mustard and thyme. Toss all together. Gently! Gently! Forty times. Less dressing and more tossing—that's the secret."

"Best salad I ever tasted in my whole life!" Bunsen proclaimed.

"A salad has to be made with *love*," Miss Roop explained to him, beaming and nodding at his compliments.

For dessert Hixie prepared cherries jubilee. "Nothing to it," she said. "Dump the cherries in the chafing dish. Throw in a blob of butter and slosh it around. Then a slurp of cognac. Oops! I slurped too much. And then . . . you light it with a match. *Voilà*!"

The blue flame leaped from the pan, and the company watched the ritual in hypnotized silence. Even Odd Bunsen was speechless.

As the flame started to burn out, Qwilleran thought he heard a crackling sound. He glanced up at Hixie and saw her lofty bouffant hairdo unaccountably shriveling. Jumping up, he tore off his jacket and threw it over her head. The women shrieked. Chairs were knocked over as Sorrel and Bunsen rushed to help.

It was a stunned and wide-eyed Hixie who emerged from under the jacket, her hands exploring what was left of her hair. "It feels like straw," she said. "I guess I sprayed too much lacquer on it."

"Come on, Bunsen," Qwilleran said. "You and I have got to go to work. Dan, are you ready?"

"Wait a minute," said the potter, walking to the head of the table. "I haven't done anything tonight—I can't cook—so I'll sing you a song."

The diners sat down and listened uncomfortably as Dan sang about the charms of Loch Lomond in a wavering tenor voice. Qwilleran watched the pathetic Adam's apple bobbing up and down and felt almost guilty about the ruse he was planning.

The song ended and the listeners applauded politely, all except Bunsen, who hopped on a chair and shouted "Bravo!" To Qwilleran he muttered: "How'm I doing?"

As the diners wandered away from the table, chattering about Hixie's narrow escape, Qwilleran helped the photographer carry his equipment in from the car.

"You fellows certainly use a lot of gear," said the potter.

"Only for big assignments like this," Bunsen said, bustling about with exaggerated industry.

"Here's what we had in mind," Qwilleran explained to Dan. "We want a series of pictures showing how you make a pot, and then a few shots of you with some of your finished work."

"Wait a minute," the photographer interrupted. "It'll never get in the paper. Who wants to look at a homely old geezer?" He gave Dan a friendly dig in the ribs. "What we need is a gorgeous blonde to jazz it up. Are you hiding any dames upstairs?"

"I know what you mean," the potter said. "You fellows always like cheesecake. But my old lady's out of town."

"How about pets? Got any cats? Dogs? Parakeets? Boa constrictors? Best way to get your picture in the paper is to pose with a boa constrictor."

"We used to have a cat," Dan said apologetically.

"Why don't we borrow one of Qwill's spoiled brats?" the photographer said with sudden enthusiasm. "We'll put him in a big jug with his head sticking out—and Dan in the background. Then you'll be sure of making the front page."

FOURTEEN

KOKO, WEARING HIS blue harness and leading Qwilleran on the twelve-foot leash, entered the pottery with the confidence of one who had been there before. There was no hesitation on the threshold, no cautious sniffing, and none of that usual stalking with underslung belly.

Qwilleran said, "Let's start by taking some shots of Dan at the wheel."

"To be honest with you fellows, I specialize in slab-built pots," Dan said. "But if that's what you want—" He scooped up a handful of clay from a barrel and sat down at the power wheel.

"Leave the cat out of this picture," Qwilleran instructed the photographer. "Just get a series of candids as the pot takes shape."

"It won't be too good," the potter said. "I've got a bad thumb." The clay started to spin, rising under his wet hands, then falling, building up to a core, lowering into a squat mound, gradually hollowed by the potter's left thumb, and eventually shaped into a bowl.

All the while, Bunsen was clicking the camera, bouncing around from one angle to another, and barking terse instructions: "Bend over . . . Glance up . . . Raise your chin . . . Don't look at the camera." And all the while, Koko was exploring the studio, nosing a clutter of mortars and pestles, crocks, sieves, scoops, ladles, and funnels. Fascinated by things mechanical, he was especially interested in the scales.

"The big story," Dan insisted, "is about my glazes. I've come up with something that's kind of cool, if you know what I mean."

"First, let's look at the clay room," Qwilleran insisted. "There may be some possibilities there for action shots."

Dan hung back. "There's nothing in that room but a lot of equipment we don't use anymore. It's all fifty, sixty years old."

"I'd like to have a look," Bunsen said. "You never know where you'll find a great picture, and I've got lots of film."

It was cold and damp in the dimly lighted clay room. Qwilleran asked intelligent questions about the blunger, pug mill, and filter press, meanwhile keeping an eye on Koko and a firm hand on the leash. The cat was attracted to a trapdoor in the floor.

"What's down there?" Qwilleran asked.

"Nothing. Just a ladder to the basement," the potter said.

The newsman thought otherwise. Joy had called it the slip tank. He leaned over and pulled up on the iron ring, swinging open the door and peering down into blackness.

A strange sound came from Koko, teetering on the edge of the square hole. It started as a growl and ended in a falsetto shriek.

"Careful!" the potter warned. "There are rats down there."

The newsman pulled Koko back and let the trapdoor fall into place with a crash that shook the floor.

"Smells pretty potent in here," Bunsen observed.

"That's the clay ripening," Dan explained. "You get used to it. Why don't we go to the kiln room? It's more comfortable, and there's not so much stink."

The high-ceilinged kiln room with its mammoth ovens and flues was pleasantly warm and clean, having neither the mud of the clay room nor the dust of the studio. On a table in the center stood a collection of square-cut vases and pots with the radiantly colorful glazes Qwilleran had glimpsed through the peephole. From a distance he had been attracted to their brilliant blues, reds, and greens; at close hand he saw that they were much more than that. There seemed to be movement in the depths of the glaze. The surfaces looked wet—and alive. The two newsmen were silent and curious as they walked around the ceramics and studied the baffling effect.

"How do you fellows like it?" asked Dan, aglow with pride. "I call it my Living Glaze."

"Sort of makes my hair stand on end," Bunsen said. "No kidding."

"Amazing!" said Qwilleran. "How do you do it?"

"Potter's secret," Dan said smugly. "All potters have their secrets. I had to work out a formula and then experiment with the fire. Cobalt oxide makes blue. Chromium oxide makes green, except when it comes out pink. You have to know your onions, if you know what I mean."

"Crazy!" said Bunsen.

"You can change colors by adding wood ash—even tobacco ash. We have a lot of tricks. Use salt, and you get orange-peel texture. I'm just giving you some interesting facts you can use in your article, if you want to make notes."

"Did Joy know you'd come up with this Living Glaze?" Qwilleran asked.

"Oh, she knew, all right!" The potter chuckled. "And it wouldn't surprise me if the old gal's nose was out of joint. Probably why she made herself scarce. She's got a pretty good opinion of herself, and she couldn't stand to see someone steal the show." He smiled and shook his head sadly.

"I like the red pots best," Qwilleran said. "Really unusual. I'm partial to red . . . So is Koko, I guess." The cat had jumped to the tabletop with the weightlessness of a feather and was gently nosing a glowing red pot.

"Red's hardest to get. You never know how it'll turn out," Dan said. "It has to get just so much oxygen, or it fades out. That's why you don't see much red pottery—honest-to-gosh red, I mean. Would you fellows like to peek in the kiln?" Dan uncovered the spyhole in one of the kilns, and the newsmen peered into the blazing red inferno. "You get so you can tell the temperature by the color of the fire," the potter said. "Yellow-hot is hotter than red-hot."

"How long does it take to fire a mess of pots?"

"Two days on the average. One day heating up, one day cooling down. Know why a dish cracks in your kitchen oven? Because your stove heats up too fast. Betcha didn't know that."

"Well, let's shoot some pictures," Bunsen said. "Dan, we'll get you standing behind the table with the crockery in the foreground. Too bad these pictures aren't in color . . . Now, we'll put Old Nosy into one of the biggest pots. You'll have to take his harness off, Qwill . . . Where's Old Nosy?"

Koko had wandered off and found a loose-leaf notebook on one of the other tables, and he was sharpening his claws on the cover.

"Hey, don't do that!" Qwilleran shouted, and then he explained: "Koko uses a big dictionary as a scratching pad—it's one of our family jokes—and he thinks that's what all books are for."

The photographer said, "You slip him in the pot, Qwill, hind feet first. Then step back out of the way and hope he stays put. Dan, you hang on to the pot so he doesn't kick it over. Old Nosy's got a kick like a mule. If he tries to jump out shove him back down. I'll shoot fast. And don't look at the camera."

Qwilleran did his part, jamming the squirming cat down into the square vase, and then he stepped away.

He missed the rest of the performance; he was curious about the notebook Koko had been scratching. The cover was labeled *Glazes*. With a casual finger Qwilleran flipped open the cover and glanced at a few words written in a familiar scrawl:

Wuu uuu 66
Quuuz 30
Cwu uuy 4

He riffled the pages quickly. Even without his glasses he recognized Joy's cryptic writing from cover to cover.

"Okay," said Bunsen. "That should do it. Old Nosy's turning into a pretty good model. What do you want next, Qwill?"

"How about some pictures of Dan in his living quarters?"

"Great!" said the photographer.

Dan protested. "No, you fellows wouldn't want to take any pictures up there."

"Sure we do. Readers like to know how artists live."

"It's a rat's nest, if you know what I mean," the potter said, still balking. "My wife isn't much of a housekeeper."

"What are you scared of?" the photographer said. "Have you got a broad up there? Or is that where you hid the body?"

Qwilleran kicked him under the table and said to Dan, "We just want to give the story a little human interest, so it won't look like a commercial plug. You know how editors are. They'll give the story more space if there's a human interest angle."

"Well, you fellows know how it's done," Dan said reluctantly. "Come on upstairs."

The Grahams' loft was one large cave, with Indian rugs on the wall, lengths of Indian fabric sagging across the ceiling, and a floor carpeted from wall to wall with old newspapers, books, magazines, half-finished sewing, and dropped articles of clothing. Crowded in that one room, without arrangement or organization, were beds, barrels, tables, kitchen sink, chairs, packing boxes covered with paisley shawls, and mop pails full of pussywillows. Two pieces of luggage were open on one of the beds.

"Taking a trip?" asked Qwilleran in his best innocent manner.

"No, just packing some of my wife's clothes to ship down south." He closed the suitcases and set them on the floor. "Sit down. Would you fellows like a beer or a shot? Us potters have to drink a lot because of the dust." He winked broadly.

"I'll take a beer," Bunsen said. "I've swallowed a little dust myself."

Qwilleran, who had carried Koko up the stairs, now placed him on the floor, and the cat hardly knew which way to turn. He stepped gingerly across a slippery stack of art magazines and sniffed a pile of clothing in odd shades of eggplant and Concord grape. They were obviously Joy's garments; they had the familiar look of old curtain remnants that had been given a homemade dye job.

The newsman plied Dan with questions: Is it true they used to glaze pottery with pulverized jewels? What's the temperature inside the kiln? Where does the clay come from? What's the hardest shape to make?

"A teapot," Dan replied. "Handles can crack in the kiln. Or the spout drips. Or the lid doesn't fit. Sometimes the whole thing looks like hell, although the ugliest ones sometimes do the best pouring."

Bunsen took a few more pictures of Dan gazing out the window at the lights across the river, Dan reading an art magazine, Dan drinking a can of beer to counteract the dust, Dan scratching his head and looking thoughtful. The photographer had never shot a series so complete, or so ridiculous.

"You've got good bones in your face," he commented. "You could be a professional model. You could do TV commercials."

"You think so?" Dan asked. He had loosened up and was relishing the attention.

By the time the shooting session was over, Qwilleran

and Koko had examined every inch of the room. There was a phone number written on a pad near the telephone, which the newsman memorized. Koko found a woman's silver-backed hairbrush, which he knocked to the floor while trying to bite the bristles. The cat also showed interest in a large ceramic jardiniere containing papers and small notebooks and a packet of dusty envelopes tied with faded ribbon. Qwilleran managed to transfer the envelopes to his inside jacket pocket. A familiar prickling sensation on his upper lip had convinced him it was the right thing to do.

The newsmen finally said good night to Dan, promised him some copies of the pictures, and trooped back to Qwilleran's apartment, dragging a reluctant cat on the leash.

"Okay, let's have it," Bunsen demanded. "What's this playacting all about?"

"Wish I knew," Qwilleran admitted. "As soon as I find out, I'll buy you a porterhouse on my expense account and fill you in on the sordid details."

"How are you going to explain to that poor guy when the *Fluxion* runs a half-column head shot and twenty words of copy?"

Qwilleran shrugged and changed the subject. "How's Janie?"

"Fine, considering everything. We're expecting another in August."

"How many have you got now?"

"Five . . . no, six."

Qwilleran poured a stiff drink for Bunsen and opened a can of crabmeat for Koko and Yum Yum. Then he dialed the number he had found on the Grahams' telephone pad. It proved to be an overseas airline.

He also thought about Joy's silver-backed hairbrush; he had given it to her for Christmas many years before. Wouldn't she have taken it if she intended to leave town? A hairbrush was as important as a toothbrush to that girl. She used to brush her long hair by the hour.

"Say," Qwilleran said to Bunsen, "do you still hang

around with that scuba diver you brought to the Press Club last winter?"

"I see him once in a while. I'm doing his wedding pictures in June."

"Would you ask him to do us a favor?"

"No sweat. He loves the *Fluxion* after that layout we gave him in the magazine section. What did you have in mind?"

"I'd like him to go down under the wharf behind this building. Just to see what he can find. And the sooner the better."

"What are you looking for?"

"I don't know, but a large unidentified object was dumped into the river in the middle of the night, and I'd like to know what it was."

"It could be halfway to Goose Island by now."

"Not necessarily. The body of the sculptor who drowned here was found lodged against the piling under the boardwalk." Qwilleran patted his mustache smugly. "I have an idea something might be trapped down there right now."

After the photographer left, the newsman sat at the desk and opened the pack of letters he had filched from the jardiniere. They were all addressed to Helen Maude Hake and had been mailed at various times from Paris, Brussels, Sydney, and Philadelphia: *I miss the thrill of you, the lure of you, you beautiful witch . . . Your warm and tender love haunts my nights . . . Home soon, beloved . . . Be true to Popsie or Popsie will spank*. All the letters were signed *Popsie*.

Qwilleran snorted into his mustache and dropped the letters in a desk drawer. He lighted his pipe and stretched out in his lounge chair, and Yum Yum cuddled on his lap—until Koko scolded her. Then she promptly deserted the man and went to lick Koko's nose and ears.

Suddenly Qwilleran felt lonely. Koko had his Yum Yum. Bunsen had his Janie. Riker had his Rosie.

He telephoned Rosemary Whiting. "I hope it's not too late. I need some moral support . . . You know those vitamins you gave me for the cats? I've never popped a pill down a cat's gullet."

Within a few minutes she knocked on the door of Number Six, wearing a red silk tunic and harem pants, with her licorice-black hair tied back in a young-looking ponytail. Qwilleran answered her knock just as Charlotte Roop climbed the stairs with a glass of steaming milk on a little tray. Miss Roop said good evening, but her greeting was cool.

The cats were waiting, and they knew something was up. They were bracing themselves.

Qwilleran said, "Let's take Koko first. He's the more sensible of the two."

"Hello, Koko," Rosemary said. "You're a beautiful cat. Here's a candy. Open up! There!" She had merely put a hand around the back of Koko's head, forced his mouth open, and dropped a pill into the yawning pink cavern. "It's really simple when you know how."

"I hate to think what will happen if Koko gets any healthier," Qwilleran said.

Just then Koko lowered his head, opened his mouth, and deposited the pellet at Qwilleran's feet. It was slightly damp but otherwise as good as new.

"Well! We'll try it again. It always works," said Rosemary, undismayed. "We'll just push it down a little farther. Qwill, you watch how I do it. Press his jaw open at the hinge; pull his head back until you can see clear down his throat; and then—*plop*! Now we stroke his throat so that he is forced to gulp."

"It looks easy," Qwilleran said, "but I think Koko is cooperating because you are a lovely lady . . . Oops!" Koko coughed, and up came the pill, shooting across the room and disappearing in the shaggy pelt of the bear rug. "Don't worry about it, Rosemary. I have a confession to make. I really lured you over here because I wanted someone to talk with."

He told her about the love letters he'd found in the jardiniere, the uncanny brilliance of Dan's exhibition pottery, and the trapdoor in the clay room. "Dan told us there were rats down there."

"Rats!" Rosemary shook her head. "Mr. Maus is very particular. He has the exterminators check the building regularly."

He told her about the visit from William's girl friend and about the peephole in the wall, overlooking the kiln room.

"But can't it be seen from the other side?"

"It's camouflaged by the mural in the kiln room. I looked for it while we were in there taking pictures."

Rosemary asked if she could read the love letters. "Believe it or not," she said, "I've never in my life received a love letter." She moved to the bed, turned on the lamp, and curled up among the pillows. As she read, her eyes grew moist. "The letters are so lovely."

On a sudden impulse Qwilleran pitched the cats into the bathroom, threw their blue cushion in after them, and slammed the door. They howled for a while and then gave up.

It was midnight when Rosemary left and the indignant animals were released from their prison. Koko stalked about the apartment, complaining irritably.

"Live and let live," Qwilleran reminded him. He was moving around the apartment himself, aimlessly, fired with ambition but devoid of direction. He sat down at the typewriter, thinking he could write a better love letter than that ridiculous Popsie. The typewriter still bore Koko's message from the night before: pb.

"Pb!" Qwilleran said aloud. "*Pb*!" He remembered the crocks in the pottery, with their cryptic labels. He jumped up and went to the dictionary as his mustache sent him frantic signals.

"Pb: Latin *Plumbum*," he read aloud. "Chemical symbol for *lead*!"

FIFTEEN

THE SECOND APPEARANCE of Qwilleran's *Prandial Musings*—in the Tuesday edition of the *Daily Fluxion*—dealt with the culinary virtuosity of Robert Maus, member of the important downtown law firm of Teahandle, Hansblow, Burris, Maus and Castle. The column was wittily written, and Qwilleran accepted congratulations from copyboys and editors alike when he went to the office to open his mail.

"How do you get these plum assignments?" he was asked at the Press Club that noon. "How much weight do you expect to gain on your new beat? . . . Do you mean to say that the *Flux* is footing the bill? The comptroller must have flipped."

He spent a day at the office, writing a column on the whimsical theories of Max Sorrel: "If you want to test a guy's sincerity," Max had said, "serve him a bad cup of coffee. If he praises it, he's not to be trusted."

In the middle of every paragraph he was interrupted, however, by phone calls: from the electric company, objecting to Maus's hotly argued preference for gas cooking; from the aluminum industry, protesting the gourmet's antipathy to foil jackets on baked potatoes; from purveyors of ketchup, processed cheese, and frozen fish, all of which made Robert Maus shudder.

One interruption was a blustering phone call from old Teahandle, senior partner of the law firm. "Did Robert Maus authorize that article in today's paper?" he demanded.

"He didn't read the finished copy," said Qwilleran, "but he allowed me to interview him."

"Humph! Are you aware that one of our major clients is a manufacturer of electric ranges?"

"Even so, Maus is entitled to his opinion, don't you think?"

"But you didn't have to *print* it!" the partner snapped. "I shall discuss this with Mr. Maus when he returns to the city."

Between answering complaints and accepting compliments, Qwilleran made some phone calls of his own. Koko had left the letter Z in the typewriter that morning, and it inspired the newsman to call Zoe Lambreth, a painter he had known briefly but well when he first came to the city. He read Zoe a list of artists' names he had copied from an old newspaper account of the scandal at the pottery.

"Are any of these people still around?" he asked.

"Some of them have died," Zoe said in the melodic voice that always captivated him. "Herb Stock has retired to California. Inga Berry is head of the pottery department at Penniman School. Bill Bacon is president of the Turp and Chisel Club."

"Inga Berry, you say? I'd like to interview her."

"I hope you're not raking up that old scandal," the painter said. "Inga refuses to talk about it. All the 'slovenly Bohemians' mentioned in the newspapers eventually became important members of the art community, and yet they're still hounded by reporters. I don't understand newspapers."

Next, Qwilleran telephoned Inga Berry, plotting his

course carefully. She answered in a hearty voice, but as soon as he identified himself as a feature writer for the *Daily Fluxion*, her manner stiffened. "What do you want?"

He talked fast and summoned all his vocal and verbal charm. "Is it true, Miss Berry, that pottery is considered the most enduring of the crafts?"

"Well . . . yes," she said, taken by surprise. "Wood crumbles, and metal corrodes, but examples of pottery have survived for thousands of years."

"I understand that pottery is due for a renaissance—that it might eclipse painting and sculpture as an art form within ten years."

"Well, I don't know . . . Well, perhaps yes!" the instructor said as she considered the flattering prospect. "But don't quote me. You'll have all the painters and sculptors yelling for my blood."

"I'd like to discuss the subject with you, Miss Berry. I have a young friend—one of your students—who paints a glowing picture of your contribution to the art of ceramics."

"Oh, he does, does he? Or is it a she?" Miss Berry was warming up.

"Do you know William Vitello?"

"He's not in my classes, but I'm aware of him." She chuckled. "He's hard to overlook."

"Have you seen him in the last couple of days?"

"I don't believe so. We haven't had any major catastrophes at the studio, so he must be absent."

"By the way, Miss Berry, is it usual to use lead in the composition of glazes?"

"Oh, yes, it's quite usual. Lead causes the pigment to adhere to the clay."

"Isn't it poisonous?"

"We take precautions, of course. Would you like to visit our studio, Mr.—Mr. . . ."

"Qwilleran, spelled with a *Q-w*. That's very kind of you, Miss Berry. I have a great curiosity about potting. Is it true that clay begins to smell bad when it ripens?"

"Yes, indeedy! The longer you keep it, the more it gains in elasticity. Actually it's decomposing."

During this conversation the receptionist in the feature department was signaling to Qwilleran; two incoming phone calls were waiting. He shook his head and waved them away.

He told the potter, "I've taken an apartment at the old pottery on River Road. It's a fascinating place. Are you familiar with it?"

There was a chilling pause on the other end of the line. "You're not going to bring up the subject of Mortimer Mellon, are you?"

"Who is he?" Qwilleran asked with an outrageous display of naiveté.

"Never mind. Forget I mentioned him."

"I was going to tell you," he said in his most engaging voice, "that my apartment has a secret window overlooking the kiln room, and my curiosity is aroused. What might its purpose be?"

There was another pause. "Which studio do you have?"

"Number Six."

"That used to be Mr. Penniman's."

"I didn't know he was an artist," Qwilleran said. "I thought he was a newspaper publisher and financier."

"He was a patron of the arts, and his studio served as a—as a—"

"Pied-à-terre?" the newsman supplied.

"You see," Miss Berry added cautiously, "I used to work in the Penniman pottery in the early days."

He expressed surprise and then inquired if she planned to attend the opening of the Graham exhibition.

"I hadn't intended to, but . . ."

"Why don't you come, Miss Berry? I'll personally keep your champagne glass filled."

"Maybe I shall. I never waste time on social openings, but you sound like an interesting young man. Your enthusiasm is refreshing."

"How will I recognize you, Miss Berry?"

"Oh, you'll know me. I have gray hair and bangs and a bit of a limp. Arthritis, you know. And of course I have clay under my fingernails."

Pleased with his own persuasiveness, Qwilleran hung up and finished the Max Sorrel column in high spirit. He handed in his copy to Riker and was leaving the office with spring in his step, when his phone rang again.

A man's voice said, "You write that column on restaurants, yeah?"

"Yes, I write the gourmet column."

"Just wanna give you some advice, yeah? Lay off the Golden Lamb Chop, yeah?"

"For what reason?"

"We don't want nothin' in the paper about the Golden Lamb Chop, y'understand?"

"Are you connected with the restaurant—*sir*?"

"I'm just tellin' you. Lay off or you're liable to lose a lot of advertisin' in the paper, yeah?" There was a click on the line.

Qwilleran reported the call to Riker. "He sounded like one of the bad guys in an old gangster movie. But now they don't threaten to bump you off; they threaten to withdraw their advertising. Did you know there's an underground movement afoot to ruin Sorrel's restaurant?"

"Ho-hum, I'll check it out with the boss," Riker said with a bored sigh. "We have your cheese column for tomorrow, and then the farmers' market piece, but we can't run what you wrote about the Petrified Bagel. 'Embalmed shrimp! Delicious toothpicks!' Are you out of your mind? What else have you lined up?"

"The Friendly Fatties. I'm going there tonight."

"Any word from Joy?"

"No word. But I'm building up a case. If I can get just one break . . ."

Qwilleran met Hixie Rice at the Duxbury Memorial Center. She was looking oddly unglamorous, despite a frizzy wig and a snugly fitted orange-and-white polka-dot ensemble.

"Do I look dumb?" she asked. "I just lost my eyelashes. I'm a loser, that's all. Everywhere except on the bathroom scales. *C'est la vie!*"

The dinner meeting of the Friendly Fatties—all sixteen tons of them—was held in a public meeting room at the center, which was noted for the mediocrity of its cuisine.

There was a brief sermon on Thinking Thin. The week's champion losers were announced, and a few backsliders—Hixie among them—confessed their sins. Then cabbage juice cocktails were served, followed by a light repast.

"Ah! Another thin soup!" Hixie exclaimed in feigned rapture. "This week they actually dragged a bouillon cube through the hot water. And the melba toast! Best I've tasted since I was a girl in Pigeon, Michigan, and ate the shingles off the barn roof . . . Do you think this is really hamburger?" she asked Qwilleran when the main course arrived. "I think it's grape seeds stuck together with epoxy glue. Don't you love the Brussels sprouts? They taste like—mmmmm—wet papier-mâché. But wait till you try the dessert! They make it out of air, water, coal tar, disodium phosphate, vegetable gum, and artificial flavoring. *Et voilà!* Prune whip!"

On the way home Hixie said, "Honestly, life is unfair. Why wasn't I born with a divine figure instead of a brilliant intellect and a ravishingly beautiful face? I can't get a man because I'm fat, and I stay fat because I can't get a man."

"What you need is a hobby," Qwilleran advised. "Some new consuming interest."

"I've got a hobby: consuming food," she said in her usual glib way, but as they walked up the stairs at Maus Haus, the happy-go-lucky fat girl burst into tears, covering her face with her hands.

"Hixie! What's the matter?" Qwilleran asked.

She shook her head and gave vent to a torrent of sobs.

He grasped her arm firmly and steered her up the stairs. "Come up to Number Six, and I'll fix you a drink."

His kind voice only made the tears gush more freely, and blindly she went along with him. Koko was alarmed at her entrance; he had never seen or heard anyone cry.

Qwilleran situated her in the big armchair, gave her a box of tissues, lit a cigarette for her, and poured two ounces of scotch over ice. "Now what's the reason for the sudden cloudburst?"

"Oh, Qwill," she said, "I'm so miserable."

He waited patiently.

"I'm not looking for a millionaire or a movie star. All I want is an ordinary, run-of-the-mill type of husband with a few brains or a little talent, not necessarily both. But do you think I ever meet that kind?" She enumerated a discouraging tally of her near-hits and total misses.

He had heard this tale of woe before. Young women often confided in him. "How old are you, Hixie?"

"Twenty-four."

"You've got lots of time."

She shook her head. "I don't think I'll ever appeal to the right kind of man. I don't want to be a swinger, but I attract men who want a swinger and nothing else. Me, I want a wedding ring, a new name, babies—all that corny stuff."

Qwilleran looked at her dress—too short, too tight, too bright—and wondered how to phrase some advice. Perhaps Rosemary could take her in hand.

"May I have another drink?" she asked. "Why is your cat staring at me?"

"He's concerned. He knows when someone's unhappy."

"I don't usually come apart like this, but I've just lived through a traumatic experience. I haven't slept for five nights. Do you mind if I tell you all the nasty details? You're so understanding."

Qwilleran nodded.

"I've just ended an affair with a married man." She paused to observe Qwilleran's reaction, but he was lighting his pipe. She went on: "We couldn't come to terms. He wanted me to go away with him, but I refused to go without making it legal. I want a marriage license. Am I a nut?"

"You're surprisingly conventional."

"But it's the same old story. He's reluctant to get a divorce. He keeps putting it off . . . Mmmm, this is good scotch. Why don't you drink, Qwill?"

"Too young."

Hixie wasn't really listening. She was intent on her own problem. "Our plans were all made. We were going to live in Paris. I was even studying French, and Dan announced—" She caught her tongue, threw Qwilleran a panicky glance.

He kept an expressionless face.

"Well, now you know," she said, throwing up her hands. "I didn't mean to let it slip. For God's sake, don't—"

"Don't worry. I'm not a—"

"I'd hate for Robert to find out. He'd have a fit. You know how he is. So proper!" She stopped and groaned with chagrin. "And Joy is a friend of yours! Ooh! I really put my foot in it this time. Promise me— Your drinks are so— Haven't slept for five— I'm so tired."

"The scotch will make you sleep well," Qwilleran said. "Shall I walk you home?"

She was a little unsteady on her feet, and he escorted her around the balcony to her own apartment just in time to say good evening to a tight-lipped Charlotte Roop, who was coming home from work.

When he returned to his own place, he found Koko busy tilting pictures.

"Stop that!" Qwilleran barked. He walked to the Art Nouveau print and took it off the hook, slid the metal plate aside, and peered through the aperture. He saw Dan toss a bundle of rags into one of the small kilns. He saw Dan look through the spyhole of a larger kiln and make a notation in a ledger. He saw Dan set an alarm clock and lie down on a cot.

Qwilleran slowly turned away from the peephole. He had recognized the rags.

SIXTEEN

QWILLERAN SKIPPED BREAKFAST Wednesday morning. He made a cup of instant coffee in his apartment and got an early start on the column about the Friendly Fatties. Koko was sitting on the desk, trying to help, rubbing his jaw on the button that changed margins, getting his tail caught in the cylinder when Qwilleran triple-spaced.

"At the Friendly Fatties' weekly dinner," the man was typing, "the Fun is more fun than the Food."

There was a knock at his door, and he found Robert Maus standing there, his round-shouldered posture looking less like a gracious bow and more like a haggard droop.

"May I violate the privacy of your sanctum sanctorum?" asked the attorney. "I have a matter of some moment, as it were, to discuss with you."

"Sure. Come in. I hear you've had an unscheduled trip out of the country. You look weary."

"Weary I am, but not, I must admit, as a result of the

unexpected detour in my itinerary. The fact of the matter is . . . that I returned to find a situation resembling mild . . . chaos."

"Will you have a chair?"

"Thank you. Thank you indeed."

The cats were regarding the visitor solemnly from the dining table, where they sat at attention, shoulder to shoulder and motionless.

"It is safe to assume," said the attorney, "that these are the two celebrated feline gastronomes."

"Yes, the big one is Koko, and the other is Yum Yum. When did you get back?"

"Late last evening, only to be confronted by a series of complications, which I will endeavor to enumerate, if I may. Whereas, three hundred persons have been invited to the opening of the pottery exhibition, and we are without a houseboy. Whereas, Mrs. Marron is suffering from allergic rhinitis. Whereas, the tennis club, our immediate neighbor to the west, has made a formal complaint about the issue of smoke from our chimneys. Whereas, the senior partner of Teahandle, Hansblow, Burris, Maus and Castle informs me that a major client has severed connections with our firm as a result of your column in yesterday's press."

"I'm sorry if—"

"The blame does not lie with you. However . . . permit me one more whereas. The esteemed Miss Roop has tendered a bill of complaint alleging scandalous conduct on the premises . . . One moment, I beg of you," Maus said when Qwilleran tried to interrupt. "It is well known to us all that the lady in question is a—you might say—bluenose. But it behooves us to humor the plaintiff for reasons best known to—"

"Never mind the preamble," Qwilleran said. "What's she objecting to?"

Maus cleared his throat and began: "To wit, one female tenant observed entering Number Six at a late hour *en négligé*. To wit, a second female tenant observed *leaving* Number Six at a late hour in a flagrant state of inebriation."

Qwilleran blew into his mustache. "I hope you don't think I'm going to dignify that gossip with an explanation."

"Explanations are neither requested nor expected—far from it," said Maus. "Let me, however, state my position. The firm with which I have the honor to be associated is of an extremely conservative bent. In the year of our Lord one thousand nine hundred and thirteen, a member of the firm was ousted from that august body—then known as Teahandle, Teahandle and Whitbread—for the simple misdemeanor of drinking three cups of punch at a garden party. I find it imperative, therefore, to avoid any suggestion of impropriety in this house. Any hint of unconventional conduct, if it reached the ears of my colleagues, would embarrass the firm, to state it mildly, and would, in all probability, relieve me of my partnership. The mere fact that I am the proprietor of what is unfortunately called a boarding house . . . places me on the brink of . . . disgrace."

"It's my guess," said Qwilleran, "that there's more unconventional conduct in Maus Haus than you realize."

"Spare me the details at the moment. When the exigencies of this day have abated, I shall—"

The telephone rang.

"Excuse me," said Qwilleran. He went to the desk and picked up the receiver. "Yes . . . Yes, what can I do for you? . . . Overdrawn! What do you mean?" He opened a desk drawer and brought out his checkbook, tucking the receiver between shoulder and ear while he found his current balance. "Seventeen-fifty! That's the wrong figure. I wrote a check for *seven*-fifty! Seven hundred and fifty dollars . . . I can't believe it. What's the endorsement? . . . I see . . . Are both signatures quite legible? . . . To be authentic, the last name in the first endorsement should look like *G-w-w-w* . . . Well, then, it's a forgery. And somebody has tampered with the amount of the check . . . Thanks for calling me. I can track it down at this end . . . No, I don't think there'll be any problem. I'll get back to you."

Qwilleran turned to his visitor, but the attorney had slipped out, closing the door. The newsman sat down and studied his next move with circumspection.

At four o'clock that afternoon the Great Hall was flooded with diffused light from the skylight three stories overhead. It fell on the jewellike objects exhibited on pedestals in the center of the floor. In this dramatic light the Living Glaze was brilliant, magnetic, even hypnotic. Elsewhere in the hall were the graceful shapes of Joy's thrown pots, bowls, vases, jars, and pitchers in subtle speckled grays and gray-greens, rough and smooth at the same time, like half-melted ice. Also on display were the brutal, primitive shapes of Dan's earlier slab pots in blackish browns and slate blues, decorated with globs of clay like burnt biscuits.

Under the balconies on both sides of the hall were long tables loaded with ice buckets, rented champagne glasses, and trays of hors d'oeuvres. The waiters were hurriedly enlisted students from the art school, awkward in white coats with sleeves too long or too short.

Qwilleran wandered through the hall and recognized the usual vernissage crowd: museum curators looking scholarly and aloof; gallery directors reserving their opinions; collectors gossiping among themselves; art teachers explaining the pots to one another; miscellaneous artists and craftsmen enjoying the free champagne; Jack Smith, the *Fluxion* art critic, looking like an undertaker with chronic gastritis; and one little old lady reporter from the *Morning Rampage* writing down what everyone was wearing.

And then there was Dan Graham, looking as seedy as ever, making a great show of modesty but bursting with vanity, his eyes eagerly fishing for compliments and his brow furrowing with concern whenever anyone asked him about Mrs. Graham.

"Helluva shame," he would say. "She's been working like a dog, and the little old gal was ready to crack up, so I sent her to Florida for some R-and-R. I don't want her to get sick. I don't want to lose her."

Qwilleran said to Graham, "The pottery racket must

be booming, if you can afford a bash like this."

Dan gave a twisted smile. "Just got a swell commission from a restaurant in L.A., with a sizable advance, so I went out on a limb for the bubble-water. Maus kicked in the snick-snacks." He jerked his head at the refreshment table, where Mrs. Marron, red-nosed and sniffling, was replenishing the supply of crab puffs, ham fritters, cheese croquettes, cucumber sandwiches, stuffed mushrooms, tiny sausage rolls, and miniature shrimp quiches.

Then Qwilleran sought out Jack Smith. "What do you think of Dan's Living Glaze?"

"I hardly know what to say. He's done the impossible," said the critic, with an expression like cold marble. "How does he get that effect? How does he get that superb red? I saw some of his pots in a group show last winter, and I said they had the character and vitality of sewer crocks. He didn't like that, but it was true. He's come a long way since then. The merit, of course, is all in the glaze. In form they're appallingly pedestrian. Those slab pots! Made with a rolling pin . . . If only they had put *his* glaze on *her* pots: I'm going to suggest that in my review."

A young girl in owlish glasses was staring at Qwilleran, and he walked in her direction.

"Was it all right for me to come here, Mr. Qwilleran?" she asked shyly. "You told me to wait forty-eight hours."

"Any word from William?"

She shook her head sadly.

"Did you check the bank account?"

"It hasn't been touched, except that the bank added twenty-six cents interest."

"Then you'd better notify the police. And try not to worry. Here, let me get you something to eat or drink."

"No, thanks. I don't feel like it. I think I'll go home."

Qwilleran escorted her to the door and told her where to catch the River Road bus.

Returning, and wandering among the crowd, he was

surprised to see the Penniman brothers. Tweedledum and Tweedledee, as they were called by irreverent citizens, seldom attended anything below the status-level of a French Post-Impressionist show.

While the other guests accorded them the deference that their wealth and name warranted, the brothers stood quietly listening, neither smoking nor drinking, and wearing the baffled expression that was their normal look at art functions. They represented the money, not the brains, behind the *Morning Rampage*, Qwilleran had been told.

He edged into the circle surrounding them and deftly maneuvered them away from the fund-raisers, job-seekers, and apple-polishers by a method known only to veteran reporters. "How do you like the show?" he asked.

Basil Penniman, the one with a cast in his left eye, looked at his brother Bayley.

"Interesting," said Bayley, at length.

"Have you ever seen a glaze like that?"

It was Bayley's turn to toss the conversational ball to Basil, whom he regarded inquiringly.

"Very interesting," said Basil.

"This is not for publication, is it?" asked Bayley, suddenly on guard.

"No, art isn't my beat anymore," said Qwilleran. "I just happen to live here. Wasn't it your father who built the place?"

The brothers nodded cautiously.

"This old building must have some fascinating secrets to tell," Qwilleran ventured. There was no reply, but he observed a faint stirring of reaction. "Before Mrs. Graham left town, she lent me some documents dealing with the early days of the pottery. I haven't read them yet, but I imagine they might make good story material. Our readers enjoy anything of a historical nature, especially if there's human interest involved."

Basil looked at Bayley in alarm.

Bayley turned pink. "You can't print anything without permission."

"Mrs. Graham promised the papers to us," said Basil.

"They're family property," said Bayley.

"They belong in the family," his brother echoed.

"We can take legal action to get them."

"Say, what's in those papers?" Qwilleran asked in a bantering tone. "It must be pretty hot stuff! Maybe it's a better story than I thought."

"You print that," said Bayley, his flush deepening to crimson, "and we'll—we'll—"

"Sue," Basil contributed hesitantly.

"We'll sue the *Fluxion*. That's yellow journalism, that's what it is!" Bayley was now quite purple.

Basil touched his brother's arm. "Be careful. You know what the doctor told you."

"Sorry if I alarmed you," Qwilleran said. "It was all in jest."

"Come," said Basil to Bayley, and they left the hall quickly.

Qwilleran was preening his mustache with wicked satisfaction when he spotted a tall, gaunt, gray-haired woman moving across the hall with halting step. "Inga Berry!" he exclaimed. "I'm Jim Qwilleran."

"Why, I was expecting a much younger man," she said. "Your voice on the phone had so much enthusiasm and—innocence, if you'll pardon the expression."

"Thank you, I think," he replied. "May I get you some champagne?"

"Why not? We'll take a quick look at the dirty old pots and then sit down somewhere and have a nice chat . . . Oh, my! *Oh, my*!" She had caught sight of the Living Glaze. She walked as quickly as she could toward the radiant display, leaning on her furled umbrella. "This is—this is better than I expected!"

"Do you approve?"

"They make me feel like going home and smashing all my own work." She drank her champagne rather fast. "One criticism: It's a shame to waste this magnificent glaze on rolled clay."

"That's what our critic said."

"He's right—for once in his life. You can tell him I said so." She stopped and stared across the hall. "Is that Charlotte Roop? Haven't seen her for forty years. Everybody ages but me."

"How about another glass of champagne?"

Miss Berry looked around critically. "Is that all they've got?"

"I have some scotch and bourbon in Number Six, if you'd care to come up," Qwilleran suggested.

"Hot dog!"

"I know you potters have to drink because of the dust."

"You scalawag!" She poked him with the umbrella. "Where did you hear that? You know too much."

She ascended the stairs slowly, favoring one knee, and when the door of Number Six was thrown open, she entered as if in a dream. "My, this brings back memories. Oh, the parties we used to give here! We were devils! . . . Hello, cats . . . Now where's this secret window you told me about?"

Qwilleran uncovered the peephole, and Miss Berry squinted through it.

"Yes," she nodded. "Penniman probably had this window cut for surveillance."

"What would he be spying on?"

"It's a long story." She sat down, groaning a little. "Arthritis," she explained. "Thank God it's in my nether joints. If it happened to my hands, I'd cut my throat. A potter's hands are his fortune. His finest tool is his thumb . . . Thank you. You're a gentleman and a scholar." She accepted a glass of bourbon. "My, this was a busy place in the old days. The pottery was humming. We had easel painters in the studios, and one weaver, and a metalsmith. Penniman had a favorite—a beautiful girl but a mediocre potter. Then along came a young sculptor, and he and the girl fell in love. He was as handsome as the dickens. They tried to keep their affair a secret, but Papa Penniman found out, and soon after that . . . well, they found the young man's body in the river . . . I'm telling you this because you're not like those other reporters. It's all ancient history now. You must be a new boy in town."

Qwilleran nodded. "Do you think his drowning was an accident, or suicide, or murder?"

Miss Berry hesitated. "The official verdict was suicide, but some of us—you won't write anything about this, will you?—some of us had our suspicions. When the reporters started hounding us, we all played dumb. We knew which side our bread was buttered on!"

"You suspected . . . Popsie?"

Miss Berry looked startled. "*Popsie*! How did you—? Well, never mind. The poor girl jumped in the river soon after. She was pregnant."

"You should have done something about it."

The potter shrugged. "What could we do? Old Mr. Penniman was a wealthy man. His money did a lot of good for the city. And we had no proof . . . He's dead now. Charlotte Roop—that woman I saw downstairs—was his secretary at the time of the drownings. She used to come to our parties, but she was a fifth wheel. We were a wild bunch. The kids today think they've invented free love, but they should have been around when *we* were young! My, it's nice to be seventy-five and done with all that nonsense . . . Hello, cats," she said again.

The cats were staring at her from their blue cushion—Koko as if he understood every word, and Yum Yum as if she had never seen a human before.

Qwilleran asked, "Why did Charlotte Roop hang around, if she didn't fit in?" He was casually lighting his pipe.

"Well, the gossips said she had a crush on her boss, and she was jealous of his beautiful paramour." Miss Berry lowered her voice. "We always thought it was Charlotte who tattled to Penniman about the affair that was going on behind his back."

"What gave you that impression?"

"Just putting two and two together. After the tragedy, Charlotte had a nervous collapse and quit her job. I lost track of her then. And if somebody didn't tip him off, why would Penniman have cut that peephole in the wall?" She leaned forward and jabbed a finger toward the newsman. "It was *just before the tragedy* that Penniman commissioned Herb Stock to paint that Egyptian-style mural in the kiln room. Now I can guess why!" Miss Berry sipped her drink and mused about the past. "Penniman was very generous with commissions, but you didn't dare cross him! You couldn't print any of this in your paper, of course."

"Not unless we wanted to start a newspaper war," Qwilleran said. It always amazed him how carelessly people spoke their minds to the press, and how surprised and indignant they were when they found themselves quoted in print.

The telephone rang.

Qwilleran picked up the receiver and said, "Hello? . . . Yes, did Odd Bunsen tell you what we want? . . . You did? Quick work! What did you find? . . . Wine bottles! Anything else? . . . What *kind* of broken crockery? . . . All of it? Wow! . . . Would you say the broken stuff was once a part of round or square pieces? . . . I see. You've been a great help. How much do I owe you? . . . Well, that's kind of you. Hope it wasn't too cold down there . . . Let me know if I can do anything for you."

Qwilleran offered to take Miss Berry to dinner, but she said she had other plans. As he accompanied her to the door he asked casually, "By the way, what happens if you heat up a kiln too fast?"

"You lose a month's work! The pots explode! It's the most heartbreaking fireworks you ever heard—pop! pop! pop!—one after the other, and it's too late to do anything about it."

Qwilleran was glad Miss Berry had other plans. He wanted to dine alone, to think. First he telephoned Dan Graham's loft and invited the potter in for a drink after dinner. To celebrate, he said. Then he went to Joe Pike's Seafood Hut.

It was a frustrating situation. Qwilleran had all kinds of curious notions that a crime had been committed but no proof—except the forged endorsement on an altered check. Added to the baffling evidence now was the frogman's report. According to his description of the "crockery" found in the river, Dan had dumped a load of broken pots. They were round pots! Joy's work, not his own. And the bright blues and greens described by the diver were the Living Glaze. Even in the muddy water, the diver said, the fragments glowed.

As Qwilleran sipped the green turtle soup, he feared that the situation was hopeless. With the baked clams he began to take heart. Halfway through the red snapper he hit upon an idea, and the salad brought him to a decision. He would take the bold step—a confrontation with Dan—and hope to expose the potter's hand. The manner of approach was the crucial factor. He was sure he could handle it.

Dan arrived at Number Six about nine o'clock, glowing with the day's success. Patting his stomach, he said, "You missed a good supper downstairs. Pork chops and some kind of mashed potatoes. I don't go for the fancy grub that Maus cooks, but the housekeeper can put on an honest-to-gosh feed when she wants to. I'm a meat-and-potatoes man myself. How about you?"

"I can eat anything," Qwilleran said over his shoulder as he rattled ice cubes. "What do you like with your bourbon?"

"Just a little ginger ale." Dan made himself at home in the big chair. "My first wife was a humdinger of a cook."

"You were married before you met Joy?"

"Yep. It didn't work out. But she sure could cook! That woman could make chicken taste like *roast beef*!"

Qwilleran served Dan his drink, poured ginger ale for himself, and made a cordial toast to the success of the potter's exhibition. Then he looked around for the cats; he always noted their reaction to visitors, and often he was influenced by their attitudes. The cats had retired behind the books on the bookshelf. He could see three inches of tail curling around a volume of English history, but it was not a tail in repose. The tip lifted in regular rhythm, tapping the shelf lightly. It meant Koko was listening. Qwilleran knew the tail belonged to Koko; Yum Yum's tail had a kink in the tip.

After Dan had quoted with relish all the compliments he had received at the champagne party, Qwilleran made a wry face and said, "I don't know whether to believe you or not."

"Whatcha say?"

"Sometimes I think you're the world's champion liar." Qwilleran used his most genial tone. "I think you're pulling my leg half the time."

"What do you mean?" Dan clearly did not know whether to grin or scowl.

"Just for example, you told me you threw the switch when Joy's hair caught in the wheel, and you saved her life. But *you* know and *I* know she never uses the electric wheel. I think you just wanted to play the big hero. Come on, now. Confess!" Qwilleran's eyes were gently mocking.

"No, you've got me all wrong! Cripes! The kick-wheel was on the blink that night, and she was rushing to finish some pots for the next firing, so she used the power wheel. There's no law against that, is there?"

"And then you told Bunsen and me there were rats in the basement; we all know that Maus had the exterminator in last month. What is this guff you're handing me?"

"Well, I'll tell you," Dan said, relaxing as he came to the conclusion that the newsman was ribbing him. "You fellows were off the track. You were trying too hard to squeeze a story out of that broken-down clay room. The real story was the Living Glaze. Am I right? No use wasting your time on stuff that isn't interesting. I know how valuable your time is. I just wanted to get you into the kiln room, that's all. Can't a guy use a little psychology, if you know what I mean?"

Qwilleran concentrated on lighting his pipe, as if it were his primary concern. "All right"—puff, puff—

"I'll buy that"—puff, puff—"but how about that cock-and-bull story that Joy is in Miami for"—puff, puff—"rest and relaxation? She hates Florida."

"I know she's always saying that, but dammit, that's where she went. This guy Hamilton is down there. I think she traipsed off to see him. They had a little thing going, you know. Joy's no saint, if you know what I mean."

"Then why didn't you ship her clothes"—puff, puff—"the way she asked? How come you burned them?" Qwilleran examined his pipe critically. "There's something wrong with this tobacco." To himself he said, Watch it, Qwill. You're on thin ice.

"So help me, they were some rags she didn't want," Dan said. "You can burn cloth in a kiln to give the pots a special hazy effect. You can pull all kinds of tricks by controlling the burning gases . . . How did you know, anyway?" Dan's eyes grew steely for a moment.

"You know how reporters are, Dan. We're always snooping around. Occupational disease," the newsman explained amiably. "Have some cheese? It's good Roquefort."

"No, I'm stuffed. Man, you nag just like my wife. You're like a dog with a bone."

"Don't let it burn you. I'm playing games, that's all. Shall I refill your glass?" Qwilleran poured Dan another drink. "Okay, try this on for size: You said you weren't taking a trip, but according to the grapevine you're heading for Paris."

"Well, I'll be jiggered! You're a nosy bugger." Dan scratched his cheek. "I suppose that nutty Hixie's been blabbing. I had to tell her *something* to get her off my neck. That kid's man-hungry, I'm telling you."

"But are you really planning to leave? I have a friend who might take over the pottery if you're giving it up."

"Just between you and me and the gatepost," the potter said, lowering his voice, "I can't warm up to this neck of the woods. I'd go back to California if I could break my contract with Maus, but I don't want to spill the beans till I know for sure."

"Is that why you broke all those pots and dumped them in the river?"

Dan's mouth fell open. "What?"

"All those blue and green pots. You can see them down there, shining right through the mud. Must be the Living Glaze."

"Oh, those!" Dan took a long swallow of bourbon and ginger ale. "Those were rejects. When I got the notion for the new glaze, I tried it out on some bisque that had sagged in the kiln. Those pots were early experiments. No point in keeping them."

"Why'd you dump them in the river?"

"Are you kidding? To save a little dough, man. The city charges by the bushel for collecting rubbish, and Maus—that old pinch-penny—makes me pay for my own trash removal."

"But why in the middle of the night?"

Dan shrugged. "Day or night, I don't know the difference. Before a show you work twenty-four hours a day. When you're firing, you check the kiln every couple of hours around the clock . . . Say, what are you? Some kind of policeman?"

"Old habit of mine," Qwilleran said; the ice was getting thinner. "When I see something that doesn't add up, I have to check it out . . . such as . . . when I write a check for seven hundred and fifty dollars and somebody ups it a thousand dollars." He regarded the potter calmly but steadily.

"What do you mean?"

"That check I gave Joy, so she could take a vacation. *You* cashed it. You should know what I mean." Qwilleran loosened his tie.

"Sure, I cashed it," Dan said, "but it was made out for seven*teen*-fifty. Joy left in a hurry, I guess, and forgot to take it with her. She'd forget her head if it wasn't fastened on. She called me from Miami and said she'd left a check for seventeen hundred and fifty dollars in the loft, and I should endorse it for her and wire her half of the money. She told me to use the rest for a big swing-ding for the opening."

"This afternoon you told me the champagne party was financed by the Los Angeles deal."

Dan looked apologetic. "Didn't want you to know she'd handed me half of your dough. Didn't want to rile you up . . . Are you sure you didn't make out that check for seventeen fifty? How could anybody add a thousand bucks to a check?"

"Easy," Qwilleran said. "Put a one in front of the numeral and add *teen* to the end of the word *seven*."

"Well, that's what she did, then, because it sure as hell wasn't me. I told you she's no saint. If you'd been married to her for fifteen years, you'd find out." Dan shifted impatiently in his chair. "Jeez! You're an ornery cuss. If I wasn't so good-natured, I'd punch you in the kisser. But just to prove there's no hard feelings, I'm going to give you a present." He pushed himself out of the deep chair. "I'll be right back, and if you want to sweeten my drink while I'm gone, that's okay with me."

That was when Qwilleran felt a tremor of uncertainty. That check he had given Joy—he had written it without his glasses and in a state of emotion. Perhaps he had made a mistake himself. He paced the floor, waiting for Dan's return.

"Koko, what are you hiding for?" he mumbled in the direction of the bookcase. "Get out here and give me some moral support!"

There was no reply, but the length of brown tail that was visible slapped the shelf vehemently.

Shortly Dan returned with two pieces of pottery: a large square urn with a footed base and a small rectangular planter. The large piece was in the rare red glaze.

"Here!" he said, shoving them across the desk. "I appreciate what you're doing for me at the paper. You said you liked red, so the big one's for you. Give the blue one to the photographer. He was a good egg. See that he gets me some copies of the pictures, will you?

. . . Well, here—take 'em—don't be bashful."

Qwilleran shook his head. "We can't accept those. They're too valuable." The red pots in the exhibition, he remembered, had been priced in four figures.

"Don't be a stuffed shirt," Dan said. "Take the damn things. I sold all the rest of the Living Glaze. People gobbled them up! I've got a stack of checks that would make you cross-eyed. Don't worry; I'll make up that thousand bucks. Just see that I get some good space in the paper."

Dan left the apartment, and Qwilleran felt his face growing hot. The confrontation had settled none of his doubts. Either he was on the wrong track entirely, or Dan was a fast-talking con man. The potter's seedy appearance was deceiving; he was slick—too slick.

There was a grunt from the bookshelves, and a cat backed into view—first the sleek brown tail, then the dark fawn haunches, the lighter body, and the brown head. Koko gave an electric shudder that combed, brushed, and smoothed his fur in one efficient operation.

"I thought I had everything figured out," Qwilleran said to him, "but now I'm not so sure."

Koko made no comment but jumped from the bookcase to the desk chair and then to the desktop. He paused, warily, before beginning to stalk the red urn. With his body low and his tail stiffened, he approached it with breathless stealth, as if it were a living thing. Cautiously he passed his nose over its surface, his whiskers angling sharply upward. His nose wrinkled, and he bared his teeth. He sniffed again, and a growl came from his throat, starting like a distant moan and ending in a hair-raising screech.

"Both of us can't be wrong," Qwilleran said. "That man is lying about everything, and Joy is dead."

SEVENTEEN

JOY HAD HATED and feared the river, and now Qwilleran was repelled by the black water beyond the window. Even Koko had shrunk from it when they explored the boardwalk. Two artists had drowned there long ago, more recently a small child, and now perhaps Joy, perhaps William. A fog was settling on the river. Boats hooted, and the foghorn at Plum Point was moaning a dirge.

Qwilleran dialed the press room at police headquarters, and while he waited for the *Fluxion* night man to come on the line, he summed up his deductions. The Living Glaze was Joy's creation; he had seen Dan copying formulas from her loose-leaf notebook into a ledger. That being true, everything else fell into place: Dan's refusal to let her show her work prior to the exhibition; the broken ceramics in the river in shapes typical of Joy's handiwork; the consensus among exhibition visitors that the glaze was too good for the clay forms beneath. Yet Dan was brazenly taking credit for the Living

Glaze. Would he dare take credit if he knew Joy was alive?

Lodge Kendall barked into the press room phone.

"Sorry to bother you again, Lodge," said Qwilleran. "Remember what I asked you about last week? I'm still interested in anything they find in the river. Where do bodies usually wash up? . . . How far is that? . . . How long does it take before they drift down to the island? It wouldn't hurt to alert the police, although I have no definite proof at this time. How about bringing Lieutenant Hames to the Press Club tomorrow? . . . Fine! See what you can do. Better still, bring him to the Golden Lamb Chop, and I'll buy . . . Yes, I *am* desperate!"

Koko was still crouched on the desktop, watching the red thing suspiciously. The small blue planter had the same fantastic glaze, yet Koko ignored it.

Cats can't distinguish colors, Qwilleran remembered. Joy had told him so. There was something else about the red urn that bothered the small animal. On the other hand, the red library book also had offended Koko; twice he had pushed it from the bookshelf to the floor.

Qwilleran found the red volume where he had wedged it between two larger books for security. It was quite a definitive book on ceramics, and Qwilleran settled down in his chair to browse through chapters on wedging clay, using the wheel, pulling a lip, beveling a foot, formulating a glaze, packing a kiln, firing a load. It ended with a chatty chapter on the history and legend of the ceramic art.

Halfway through the last chapter Qwilleran felt nauseated. Then the blood rushed to his face, and he gripped the arms of the chair. In anger he jumped up, strode across the room, and swung the book at the red pottery urn, sweeping it off the desk. The cats fled in alarm as the urn shattered on the ceramic floor tiles.

Still gripping the book, Qwilleran lunged out of the apartment and around the balcony to Number One. Robert Maus came to the door, tying the belt of a flannel robe.

"Got to talk to you!" Qwilleran said abruptly.

"Certainly. Certainly. Please come in. I presume you have heard the midnight newscast: a bomb scare at the Golden Lamb Chop . . . My dear fellow, are you ill? You are shaking!"

"You've got a madman in the house!" Qwilleran blurted.

"Sit down. Sit down. Calm yourself. Would you accept a glass of sherry?"

Qwilleran shook his head impatiently.

"Some black coffee?"

"Dan has murdered his wife! I know it, I know it!"

"I beg your pardon?"

"And probably William, too. And I think Joy's cat was the first victim. I think the cat was an experiment."

"One moment, I beg of you," said Maus. "What is this incoherent outburst? Will you repeat it? Slowly, please. And kindly sit down."

Qwilleran sat down as if his knees had collapsed. "I'll take that black coffee."

"It will require only a moment to filter a fresh cup."

The attorney stepped into his kitchenette, and Qwilleran gathered his thoughts. He was in better control when Maus returned with the coffee. He repeated his suspicions: "First, the Grahams' cat disappeared; then Joy disappeared; then William. I say he has murdered them all. We've got to do something!"

"This is a preposterous accusation! Where is your proof, if I may ask?"

"There's no tangible proof, but I *know*!" Qwilleran touched his mustache nervously; he thought it better not to mention Koko's behavior. "In fact," he said, "I'm going to see a homicide detective tomorrow."

Maus raised a hand. "One moment! Let us consider the consequences before you speak to the authorities."

"Consequences? You mean adverse publicity? I'm sorry, Maus, but publicity is inevitable now."

"But pray what brings you to the . . . monstrous conclusion that Graham has . . . has—"

"Everything points to it. For years Joy has been outshining her husband. Now she formulates a spectacular glaze that will allow her to eclipse him completely. The man has a sizable ego. He desperately wants attention and acclaim. The solution is simple: Why not get rid of his wife, apply her glaze to his own pottery, and take the credit? The marriage is falling apart anyway. So why not? . . . I tell you it's true! And once Joy was out of the way, Dan took the precaution of destroying all her pottery that carried the new glaze. We found the stuff—"

"You must pardon me if I say," the attorney interrupted, "that this . . . this wild scenario sounds like a figment of an overwrought imagination."

Qwilleran ignored the remark. "Meanwhile, Dan discovers that William suspects him, and so the houseboy must be silenced. You have to admit that William has been conspicuously absent."

The attorney stared in disbelief.

"Furthermore," the newsman went on, "Dan is preparing to leave the country. We've got to act fast!"

"One question, if you please. Can you produce the prime evidence?"

"The bodies? No one will ever find them. At first I thought he'd dumped them in the river. Then I found a sickening fact in a book—in *this* book." Qwilleran shook the red volume at his incredulous listener. "In ancient China they used to throw the bodies of unwanted babies into the pottery kilns."

Maus made no move. He looked stunned.

"Those kilns downstairs can heat up to twenty-three hundred degrees! I repeat: The bodies will never be found."

"Ghastly!" the attorney said in a whisper.

"You remember, Maus, that the tennis club complained about the smoke last weekend. And William knew something was wrong. Ordinarily pots take twenty-four hours for firing and twenty-four for cooling. If you speed it up, they explode! William told me Dan was firing too fast. The pottery door was locked, but William knew about the tiny window in Number

Six, overlooking the kiln room . . . Do you know about the peephole?"

Maus nodded.

"And there's another story in this book," Qwilleran said. "It happened centuries ago in China. A barnyard animal wandered into a kiln while it was being loaded. The animal was cremated, and the clay pots emerged in a glorious shade of *red*!"

The attorney looked acutely uncomfortable.

"Joy's cat was probably the first experiment," Qwilleran added.

Maus said, "I feel unwell. Let us discuss this in the morning. I must think."

That night Qwilleran found it impossible to sleep. He was up, he was down, he tried to read, he walked back and forth in the apartment. Koko was also awake and alert, watching the man with concern. For one brief moment Qwilleran considered a knockout shot of whiskey, but he caught Koko's eye and desisted. Eventually he remembered some cough syrup in the medicine cabinet. It contained a strong sedative. He took a double dose.

Soon he was sleeping too deeply to dream. The foghorn continued to moan, and the boats hooted their continual warnings, but he heard nothing.

Suddenly he catapulted out the depths of his drugged sleep and found himself sitting up in the dark. In his groggy state he thought there had been an explosion. He shook his head, remembered where he was. A kiln! That's what it was, he told himself. A kiln had exploded. He switched on the bed lamp.

There had been no explosion—only the fall of a body, the crash of a chair, the crack of a head hitting the ceramic tile floor, the shattering of a window. On the floor, his head bloodied, lay Dan Graham, his legs sprawled across a tangle of gray yarn. The room was crisscrossed with yards and yards of gray strands, like a giant spiderweb.

On the bookcase sat Koko, his ears back and his slanted eyes shining red in the lamplight.

* * *

"And that's how it happened," Qwilleran explained to Rosemary when she dropped in at Number Six before dinner on Thursday. He was wearing his new suit for the first time, planning to take Rosemary to the Golden Lamb Chop, and the scale indicated he was ten pounds lighter. He also felt ten years younger.

"Koko had booby-trapped the apartment with your ball of yarn," he said, "and Dan tripped over it in the dark."

"How do you know Koko spun the web?" Rosemary asked. "More likely it was Yum Yum."

"I bow to your feminine intuition. Forgive my chauvinism."

"What was Dan going to attack you with? One newscaster called it a blunt weapon. The newspaper said it was a wooden club."

"You'd never believe it, but it was a rolling pin! A heavy wooden one that potters use to roll clay for slab pots. When Dan stumbled into the booby trap, the rolling pin flew out of his grasp and broke a window."

Rosemary shook her head in wonder. "He wasn't a brainy man, but he was crafty, and I'm surprised he thought he could get away with it."

"He was all ready to leave the country. The Renault was packed and ready to leave for an early morning flight. He wasn't even going to hang around to read the reviews of his show."

The cats had just finished eating a beef and oyster pâté sent up by Robert Maus, and now they were sitting on the desk, washing faces and paws in an aura of absolute contentment. Qwilleran regarded them with pride and gratitude. He remembered the *pb* on the page in the typewriter.

"I was wrong about one detail," he went on. "They found William's body. If Dan had committed only one murder, he could have risen to fame with Joy's glazes. But when he spiked William's drink with lead oxide, he was in trouble. He couldn't dispose of William's body in the kiln; it was full of pots in the cooling stage. So he stored it in the slip tank in the basement of the clay room."

There was a knock on the door, and Qwilleran opened it to admit Hixie.

"Did I hear the rattle of ice cubes?" she asked.

"Come in. We'll open the bottle of champagne the Press Club sent to Koko. And Yum Yum," Qwill added, with an apologetic glance at Rosemary.

Hixie said, "I wonder how Teahandle, Hansblow, Et Cetera, Et Cetera reacted to the publicity? Television and everything! I'll bet Mickey Maus is in the soup."

"It's a blessing in disguise," said Rosemary. "Now he'll retire from law and do what he has always wanted to do—open a restaurant."

There was another knock at the door—a positive, urgent, angry knock. Charlotte Roop was standing there with tense lips and clenched fists. She marched into the apartment with aggressive step and announced, "Mr. Qwilleran, I would like a drink. A strong drink! A glass of *sherry*!"

"Why . . . certainly, Miss Roop. I think we have sherry. Or would you like champagne?"

"I need something to quiet my nerves." She put a trembling hand to her flushed throat. "I have just resigned from the Heavenly Hash House chain. I resigned in moral indignation!"

"But you liked your job so much!" Rosemary protested.

"What happened?" Qwilleran asked.

"The three owners," Charlotte began, her voice beginning to quaver, "the men I respected so highly have been engaged in the most disreputable maneuver I have ever encountered in the business world. I overheard a conversation—quite by accident, of course—in the conference room . . . Is this champagne? Thank you, Mr. Qwilleran." She took a cautious sip.

"Well, go on," said Hixie. "What have they been doing? Watering the soup?"

Charlotte looked flustered. "How can I tell you? It pains me to mention it . . . *They* are the ones who have been trying to ruin Mr. Sorrel's restaurant!"

"But they're not in the same league," Qwilleran protested. "The Hash Houses don't compete with the Golden Lamb Chop."

"The Golden Lamb Chop," Charlotte explained, "occupies a very valuable corner, with exposure to three major highways. The Hash House syndicate, through brokers, has been trying to buy it, but Mr. Sorrel would not sell. So they resorted to unscrupulous tactics. I am horrified!"

"Would you testify in court?" Qwilleran asked.

"Yes indeed! I would testify even if their gangster friends threatened to—threatened to—"

"Waste you," Hixie said. "A five-letter word meaning 'to bump off.' "

"If Mr. Maus opens a restaurant, you can manage it for him," Rosemary said.

The voices of the three women rambled on, and Qwilleran listened with bemused inattention. He liked the gentle-voiced Rosemary; he felt comfortable with her, and comfort was beginning to be of utmost importance. His emotional but brief reunion with Joy had been a misstep in the march of time, and now her memory was relegated to the past, where it belonged. He doubted, however, that he would ever again say that his favorite color was red.

There was a click on the desk, and he looked up to see Koko walking across the typewriter keyboard.

"Look!" Hixie squealed. "He's typing!"

Qwilleran walked over and looked at the sheet of paper. He put on his glasses and looked again. "He's ordering a bite to eat," the newsman said. "Since we moved to Maus Haus, he has learned to like caviar."

Koko had stepped on the *K* with his right paw, on *V* with his left, and then on the *R*.

The Cat Who Played Brahms

Lilian Jackson Braun

Is it just a case of summertime blues or a full-blown career crisis? Newspaper reporter Jim Qwilleran isn't sure, but he's hoping a few days in the country will help him sort out his life.

With cats Koko and Yum Yum for company, Qwilleran heads for a cabin owned by a long-time family friend, 'Aunt Fanny'. But from the moment he arrives, things turn strange. Eerie footsteps cross the roof at midnight. Local townsfolk become oddly secretive. And then, while fishing, Qwilleran hooks on to a murder mystery. Soon Qwilleran enters into a game of cat and mouse with the killer, while Koko develops a sudden and uncanny fondness for classical music . . .

Qwilleran – a prize-winning reporter with a nose for crime. Koko – a Siamese cat with extraordinary talents and a flair for mystery. Yum Yum – a loveable Siamese adored by her two male companions. The most unlikely, most unusual, most delightful team in detective fiction!

0 7472 5036 7

HEADLINE

The Cat who Blew the Whistle

Lilian Jackson Braun

Jim Qwilleran and his Siamese sleuths are back in another crime-busting adventure.

When the residents of Moose County, including the reclusive millionaire, Jim Qwilleran, board the old steam locomotive – the celebrated Engine No. 9 – on its inaugural journey, little do they know that this first trip will also be the last . . .

By next morning, Qwill discovers that the affluent owner of Engine No. 9, Floyd Trevelyn, has disappeared, along with his glamorous secretary and millions of dollars belonging to Moose County investors.

While the search is on for the fugitive, Qwill stays in Pickax and probes another mystery – why has Koko developed a sudden interest in certain works of literature and started to steal black pens?

0 7472 4815 X

HEADLINE